Fern Britton

The Great Cornish Getaway

HarperCollins*Publishers* Ltd
1 London Bridge Street,
London SE1 9GF

www.harpercollins.co.uk

First published by HarperCollins*Publishers* 2018
1

A catalogue record for this book is available from the British Library

ISBN: 9780008264611

This novel is entirely a work of fiction.
The names, characters and incidents portrayed in it are
the work of the author's imagination. Any resemblance to
actual persons, living or dead, events or localities is
entirely coincidental.

Typeset in ITC Stone Serif by
Palimpsest Book Production Ltd, Falkirk, Stirlingshire

Printed and bound by CPI Group (UK) Ltd, Croydon CR0 4YY

MIX
Paper from
responsible sources
FSC™ C007454

This book is produced from independently certified FSC™ paper
to ensure responsible forest management.
For more information visit: www.harpercollins.co.uk/green

To all new readers,
I hope you have fun x

Chapter 1

Richard was cold.

Cold and wet.

His silver hair, wet with raindrops, flopped over his forehead as he hunched into his tweed overcoat, and turned against the wind and penetrating rain. God, but England could be miserable in the winter.

He should be in Massachusetts, but here he was, spending ten days in the UK. A very old friend had persuaded him to make a cameo appearance in a film directed by a young whizz-kid who needed a leg up the Hollywood ladder.

He hadn't wanted to do it. He'd had a busy year and was in need of a break.

Physically and mentally.

It was a mess.

The director didn't know her arse from her elbow and the crew were just as clueless. He was losing patience, and his cold, which had set in on the flight over from LA, filled his nose, ears and brains.

He was not a happy man.

* * *

Tizzy, the director, had finished bossing everyone around and was ready at last.

'Here we go and . . . *action*.'

Richard opened his mouth but, to his embarrassment, no words came out.

'Cut!' shouted Tizzy impatiently. She stomped up to him. 'What is the matter?'

He smiled as nicely as he could. 'Sorry, I forgot the line.'

'Got it now? Or do you want Sadie to give you the script, again?'

'No, no. It's fine.' His patience was almost lost, but he hung onto it.

She turned and walked quickly back to her position. He heard her tutting to Jango, 'He forgot his fricking lines. I knew we should have got Jim Broadbent.' She looked at Richard as if he was stupid. 'Sure you're OK, Rich?'

He smiled tightly.

'Good. And, *action*.'

He delivered the line, and he knew he'd got the thought behind it and the delivery spot on.

'Keep rolling and let's do it again, before we lose the light. Try and give us a smile at the end of the line, Rich,' Tizzy shouted.

They did it seven more times. Each time she asked for a different tone or expression. At last the crew told her the light had gone for the day.

Richard gladly put on his coat and headed back towards his trailer.

Instead of following the path to his trailer, though, he turned his collar up and looked for the footpath he knew would get him to the main road.

It ran between two high hedges and smelt of rotting greenery.

Walking now down the dark road, Richard tried to get his brain to think sensibly and make a plan. But it was impossible. He just knew he had to get as far away from the set as possible.

When he heard a car coming from behind, he pulled his collar up and walked into the shadows.

The car slowed, moving at his pace. He heard the purr of an electric window.

'Mr Gere? Richard? You OK?'

Richard stopped walking and the car stopped too. He looked at his driver, Kevin, sitting warm in his comfortable car.

'I don't want to go back,' he said.

'To the hotel?' Kevin asked.

Richard looked at his shoes and didn't answer.

'Where do you want to go?' Kevin said.

'Away from here.'

'Fair enough. Any ideas?'

'How far are we from Cornwall?' Richard asked after a pause.

Kevin laughed. 'A bloody long way.'

Just before midnight June, Kevin's wife, saw her husband's car turn onto the driveway of their neat 1930s semi. She watched as Kevin got out and opened the back door for his passenger.

'Oh, blimey, Butler,' June said to her little dog as the passenger got out. 'It bloody well *is* Richard Gere.'

She ran to the kitchen to put the kettle on, and then to the front door to let Kevin and their visitor in.

'Hello. Do come in. Make yourself at home. I've got the kettle on.'

Richard shook her hand. 'I'm so sorry to land on you like this, but Kevin insisted it would be OK.'

The boiled kettle beeped from the kitchen. 'Of course it's OK. We're not the Dorchester but I do a nice pot of tea. Give me your coat.'

Richard walked into the homely comfort of the living room. Family photos on the mantelpiece. A large chintz sofa and two matching armchairs. An enormous television in the corner and a pair of glamorous velvet curtains at the bay window.

June came in carrying a tray crammed with small side plates, dainty sandwiches and a Battenberg cake. 'I wasn't sure if you'd be hungry, but you'll sleep better with a full tummy. Kevin, come and get the tea tray, would you, please?'

Sitting on the sofa and taking in the wonderful normality, Richard began to relax. Tomorrow he'd call his agent and tell her he was fine. He just needed to take some time out. No big deal. Actors walked off films all the time.

June sat back with her best cup and saucer. 'Kev says you want to go to Cornwall.'

'I have old friends there who I haven't seen for far too long.'

'Of course, you helped to save the old Pavilions theatre with that film. We've been once or twice since it was renovated, haven't we, Kev? It's really special now. Your photo is up on the wall in the foyer. Pride of place.'

'You've been to Trevay?' Richard asked, amazed.

'Well, yes.' June passed him a plate of chocolate biscuits. 'Kev and I have a caravan just about ten minutes away. Rocky Cliffs Holiday

Park. It's lovely. We bought it when the kids were small. Do you know Rocky Cliffs?'

Kevin tutted. 'Why would he know a caravan park? I expect he stayed at the Starfish.'

Richard munched his biscuit and tickled the dog, Butler. 'I have stayed at the Starfish. A lovely hotel.'

'Well, you can't stay at the Starfish this time, can you?' said Kevin. 'Not if you want to stay away from people and cameras. Can you stay with your friends?'

June suddenly clutched Kevin's arm. 'I've had a thought. Why don't you take Richard down to the caravan? No one will go looking for him there. It's ever so quiet at this time of year. It's the last place they'd think of.'

'I'd love to stay there.'

'Are you sure?' Kevin asked uncertainly.

June stopped him. 'It's just what he needs. Look how relaxed *you* get when you're there. I reckon a bit of sea air away from the nutters will do you good.' She looked from one man to the other and made their minds up for them. 'That's sorted then. You can go tomorrow. You need a good night's sleep first, though. You've both had a long day, and look at the time! The middle of the night. Kev, take Richard up to his room and show him the bathroom.'

Richard stood up. 'I can't thank you enough, June. I feel better than I have for days.' He gave her a hug and kissed her cheek. She noted his distinctive scent of cologne. Heavenly.

'Oh. Well. It's our pleasure,' she said.

'Can I help you with these trays and the washing-up?' he asked.

'No, no. Off to bed with you. Go on. I won't be long.'

June watched as her husband and the handsome film star climbed the stairs. Then she went to the kitchen to load the dishwasher. Finally she let Butler out for a last wee, and saw her reflection in the kitchen window. 'Oh, June,' she said, touching her cheek. 'You've just been kissed by Richard Gere.'

Chapter 2

In the Cornish village of Pendruggan, the early morning sun was shining brightly.

At the Dolphin pub, the landlady, Dorrie, had cleaned the bar and the lavatories. She was now upstairs in her favourite armchair with a cup of coffee and the newspaper waiting by her side. This was one of her favourite times in the day; the place was her own, at least until the lunchtime drinkers arrived.

The old pub settled around her as she closed her eyes and sipped her coffee.

Her two boys were at sea working on the fishing boats. They wouldn't be home until the end of the week. Don, her husband, was building a conservatory for some second-home owners in Trevay.

She opened her eyes and looked happily on the lane winding down to the village. Twists of woodsmoke came from several chimneys, and a couple were walking their dogs on the green. The Atlantic Ocean sparkled beyond. All was well with the world.

She picked up the day's paper by her side and took another sip of coffee before reading the headline.

'FILM ACTOR RICHARD GERE IS
MISSING'

She almost choked.

At the vicarage, on the other side of the village green, Penny was enjoying the quiet of her kitchen. Her husband, Simon, was across the hall in his study asking for divine guidance as he typed out his Sunday sermon. She should be in her own office, opposite Simon's, working on the budget for a new project.

But instead she rummaged in her bag for her phone and gave in to the guilty pleasure of checking Twitter. She checked her news app first.

Moments later she crashed open Simon's office door.

'Richard has disappeared,' she announced.

'Richard?' said Simon vaguely. 'Richard at the garage?'

'No, no,' said Penny, her voice rising with impatience, 'Gere. Richard Gere.'

'How do you know?'

9

'It's all over the news.'

'I thought you were working?'

'Never mind that.' Penny showed her husband the phone. 'Look. He's been filming here in the UK.'

'Whereabouts?' asked Simon with interest.

Penny huffed crossly, 'Does it matter?'

'I'd like to know, that's all. If it's local then maybe I could find him.'

'Northumberland,' Penny said, slumping into the nearest armchair.

'Oh,' said Simon. 'That's a long way from Cornwall.'

'Perhaps he's seriously ill? Or having a nervous breakdown?'

'Now you're being too dramatic,' said Simon. Richard and Penny had bonded thanks to his help with her TV production studio a few years ago. It was a close friendship and, as with all her good friends, Penny was fiercely protective of Richard.

Penny had an idea. 'Maybe it's a brilliant PR trick? You know, to get people interested in the film?'

'Maybe.' Simon squinted at the sermon on his computer screen.

Penny huffed again.

The phone rang.

Neither of them moved. It was bound to be someone in the parish asking about the harvest festival.

They listened as Simon's recorded message played. *This is Pendruggan vicarage, the Reverend Simon Canter speaking. I am so sorry I am unable to take your call but do please leave a message and I'll get back to you. Thank you for calling.*

Whoever it was paused before hanging up.

'I wonder who that was?' asked Simon.

'Who cares?' said Penny. 'Richard is more important right now. I hope he's OK. It's a long time since we heard from him.'

'We had a Christmas card. He knows where we are if he needs us,' said Simon wisely. 'Did the news give any clues?'

'Just that he's been missing since yesterday morning. His agent has said that he is taking some time out. The film company are saying they may sue him for breach of contract.'

Simon turned back to his sermon. 'He'll turn up.'

Chapter 3

Richard and Kevin had arrived at Rocky Cliffs Holiday Park the evening before. They'd had a long journey, made easier by the spare clothes and cologne that Richard kept in a bag in the car.

It had been dark when they'd arrived, but the caravan was just as June had promised – brightly furnished and comfortable. Kevin turned on the central heating and emptied the car. He showed Richard to the double bedroom with en suite bathroom. 'This will be you, and I'm next door in the kids' room. No arguing! Fancy fish and chips for supper? I'll nip into the village to get some, and in the meantime, there's a bottle of wine in the fridge. Help yourself.'

Richard slept well again that night. He woke up to the sound of seagulls tap-dancing on the roof and the smell of bacon frying. He looked at his watch – 6.30 a.m.

'Morning,' said Kevin. 'Sleep well?'

'You bet.' Richard stretched and yawned. 'Want me to open the curtains or are there too many people about?'

'Mate, the place is dead. Go ahead. Draw the curtains. I think you'll like what you see.'

'Oh my goodness.' Richard was stunned as he pulled the flowery curtains across the picture window. The caravan was on the top of a cliff looking out over a vast horizon. The sun was rising and glinted off an inky sea. 'It's gorgeous. Is that the Atlantic?'

'Yep.'

'There's someone out there, surfing. It's really early and it's February. Are they mad?'

'Yes, but it's almost a religion down here. Would you like to have a go?'

'Oh sure. I mean, I'm only an American who is used to the warm waters of the Atlantic or the Caribbean. I'd really love to freeze my butt off in that!'

Kevin laid the neat dining table with some cutlery and two mugs of tea. 'You want some toast?'

'I want to go walk on that beach.'

'Have your breakfast and we will.'

After breakfast, while Kevin had a shower, Richard slipped out for a walk on the cliffs to see if he could catch a phone signal. Finally, high on a blowy cliff, his phone showed a few signal bars, and he made a quick call to let his nearest and dearest know that he was all right.

By the time he got back to the caravan he was feeling better than he had in days. The voices of home had soothed him.

As he stepped inside the caravan, the first thing he heard was his name.

Kevin was watching the television and Richard was the main topic of conversation. The presenters were trying to guess where he could have gone and why.

Kevin was suddenly aware Richard was behind him. 'Well, they know you've done a bunk now.' He turned the television off. 'You OK?'

Richard sat down heavily on the plump sofa. The good mood of just a few minutes ago was slowly fading. Putting his head in his hands, he swore softly to himself.

'What are we going to do? Would you like me to take you back?' Kevin asked.

Richard thought for a moment. 'Can you cut my hair?'

'What?'

'Can you cut my hair? Real short?'

'I doubt it, and if I do it'll look terrible.'

'Great. Got any scissors?'

'I think June has some kitchen ones, or I've got nail clippers.'

Richard got up and searched June's cutlery drawer. 'Here,' he said, holding up a pair of scissors so large you could cut carpet with them. 'These are fine.'

Richard took off his jumper and T-shirt and pulled up a chair. 'Do it.'

'How short?'

'I don't care. Just make me look different.'

'OK.' Kevin gingerly took a lock of the famous snow-white hair. 'Ready?'

'Uh-huh.'

'Here goes.' He took the first snip.

Twenty minutes later Richard looked in the mirror. 'Wow. That's good.'

Kevin was unsure. 'It's very short.'

Richard ran his hand over his stubbly head. 'It's perfect. Have you got any old clothes I can borrow? My new ones will stand out.'

'Yes, but they're all rather shabby.'

'Go get them.'

Kevin searched out a pair of ripped and faded jeans. A salt-stained T-shirt. A well-worn hoodie and a battered baseball cap. 'These any good?' he asked.

Richard tried them on. He was a little smaller

than Kevin, which gave the whole outfit a better look. 'I love this hat.'

'It's my fishing hat. Don't lose it. It has sentimental value,' Kevin joked.

Richard adjusted the clothes and hat, and then put on his glasses. 'There, how do I look?'

'Like a local.'

'Do you think people will recognise me?'

Kevin gave him a full head-to-toe survey.

'As long as you don't speak, you'll be fine.'

'Have you forgotten I'm an actor?' asked Richard. 'Listen.' He cleared his throat and then said in a West London voice, 'How now, brown cow.'

Kevin was amazed. 'Not bad. Not bad at all. Where did you learn that?'

'I lived in London in 1973. Worked in the West End doing *Grease*.'

'*Grease*?'

'The musical. Before John Travolta made the movie, I played his part. Danny Zuko.'

'You did?'

'Yep, and while I was over here I practised the accent. It's come in useful once or twice.'

'Blimey, mate, it had bloody better do the job now, or you're busted.'

'OK, let's go to Trevay and grab a coffee.'

As Kevin picked up his car keys, Richard

asked, 'Can you teach me how to talk like you? Some of that cockney slang?'

'Of course, me old china plate. Lesson one starts as soon as we get on the frog and toad.'

As Kevin and Richard drove to Trevay, the rest of the country was waking up to newspapers running pages and pages of photos of Richard; then and now. Details of his work and love affairs. Comments from 'film buffs', 'close friends' and leggy young women – all keen to get themselves in the paper whether they had met him or not.

Chapter 4

A gang of reporters arrived outside the vicarage, taking it in turns to bang on the door and shout through the letter box.

Dorrie was furious. 'I'm ringing Don. He'll come and thump them.'

Simon was alarmed. 'No need for that. I'll go out and reason with them.'

Penny was alarmed now. 'No, you won't. Anyway, it's cold out there.'

'Penny, it'll be fine.' He reached for his fleece. 'I'll be back in a minute.'

As Simon opened the front door, he met a storm of questions from the pack outside. Penny and Dorrie dodged out of sight into his office and peeked through the curtains.

Simon was holding his hands up to silence the gang. 'Good morning . . .'

But before he could go on a voice shouted, 'What's your name?'

'I am Simon Canter. Vicar of this parish. I assume you want to know where Richard Gere is?'

'Is he hiding in the church?' called an old hack from the back. The others sniggered.

Simon tried to regain control. 'My wife and I have no idea where Richard is, but he is most definitely not here.'

'Are you concerned about his disappearance?' asked a wide-eyed young reporter from the *Daily Mirror* holding a tape recorder towards Simon.

'Well, of course we are worried, but he has many friends and he knows he's welcome here.'

A television cameraman was standing at the back of the small crowd and filming everything.

'And your wife?' asked the girl from the *Daily Mirror* again. 'How is she?' she asked with a suspicious tone, unaware of the simple friendship between Penny and Richard.

'Like anyone, she is very concerned and upset.'

'Do you have a message for Mr Gere if he's watching?' shouted a voice.

Simon hesitated. 'Richard, wherever you are, I hope you know that a lot of people are worried for you and . . .' He hadn't time to finish. The front door behind him flew open and Penny grabbed his arms. She pulled him back into the house and slammed the door in the faces of the press.

'Ow,' he said, rubbing his arms. 'What did you do that for?'

'There's a television camera shooting the whole thing. You've just given the press the best soundbite they'll get today. How could you?'

Simon's expression turned from pain to horror to apology. 'Oh.'

'Yes, OH!' shouted Penny. 'I told you not to go out there.'

Dorrie looked at her watch. 'I'd better get back to the pub for opening. I'll go out the back way. Call me if you get any news.'

'Likewise,' said Penny, kissing her friend.

As she watched Dorrie climbing over the garden wall and edging around the graveyard to avoid the press, her mobile pinged with a text. It was from her best and oldest friend Helen.

I've just seen the news. I'm coming over.

Penny replied. *Come through the back door. Reporters at the front. We are under siege!!!!*

Helen shut the front door of her cottage – which was called Gull's Cry – and looked across the village green to the vicarage. There were several strange cars, a couple of Range Rovers and a BBC Cornwall radio car. By the front gate a group of men and women were either on their phones, stamping their feet, smoking, or doing all three.

Penny was waiting for her in the kitchen. 'Coffee?'

'Yes, please. How long have those idiots been outside for?'

'A couple of hours.'

'Really? What do they think they're going to get?'

'God knows. Come into the lounge. Simon may be on the telly in a minute.'

On the sofa, Simon was sitting, ashen-faced, watching himself give his surprise press conference.

'Oh God,' said Penny, sitting down heavily next to him.

'Shit,' said Helen under her breath as she sat in an armchair.

'I'm so sorry.' Simon blinked behind his glasses.

Penny put an arm around him and squeezed. 'You weren't to know,' she said, aware of how her relationship with Richard may have been misjudged.

21

Chapter 5

Just below the Starfish Hotel, Kevin was parking the car in the harbour car park. Richard nudged Kevin and pointed up to the headland above the village. 'There she is. The reason I came here in the first place.'

Kevin looked at the familiar silver dome of the 1950s ice cream-coloured theatre. 'The old Pavilions,' he said, smiling. 'June and I went last summer. The local theatre group put on *Annie Get Your Gun*. Really good, it was.'

'I'm glad to hear it. Give me some change and I'll get a parking ticket.'

'You sure?'

'Sure I'm sure. Who'd recognise me with this haircut and outfit?'

Kevin watched as Richard strolled to the ticket machine. The harbour master and another man were walking towards the harbour master's office. They looked at Richard and then ignored him.

Kevin relaxed, and then watched as Richard fumbled with the unfamiliar coins and the machine. Successful, he returned smiling and gave the ticket to Kevin. 'That's for the jar parking.'

Kevin shook his head. 'Haven't you been listening to me? You don't say "jar", you say "jam". Car rhymes with jar, but to confuse the old bill you say "jam" for jam jar.'

'The old bill?' asked Richard.

'Shut your gob and cover your barnet and your boat with my titfer.'

Richard stopped in his tracks and started to laugh. 'Stop, stop. What are you saying to me? You're making it up.'

Kevin sighed. 'We've got a lot of work to do,' he said. 'Come and get a coffee and stop drawing attention to yourself.'

They walked towards the Sail Loft café, a new coffee house and wine bar on a side street away from the harbour. On the way Richard pulled out his phone and saw he had a signal. Kevin was outside the newsagent's and about to go in. 'I'll wait for you out here,' said Richard. 'Just going to make a call.'

Richard scrolled down his contacts list. He was going to try phoning Simon and Penny again. When he'd phoned earlier he'd been put off by the answer phone. Maybe they were away? He'd try again. But before he could, Kevin came out of the newsagent's looking worried, with several newspapers in his hand. Richard hung up without leaving a message. 'What's the matter, Kev?'

Kevin unfolded two of the front pages while looking around to make sure no one was watching. 'You're on every bloody front page, mate.'

Richard felt the world tilt a little under his feet. What had he started? All he'd wanted was some peace and a moment to step out of his life, and now he was being hunted? He drew a deep breath. He had three choices. Run and hide. Turn up again and apologise. Get a coffee and think.

'Come on, let's get that coffee.' He slung his arm around Kevin's shoulder and together they walked to the Sail Loft.

Inside it was warm and comforting. A group of young women with babies was at one table juggling cappuccinos with breastfeeding. The women glanced up to check out the two older men as they came in.

What they saw was a bald man with a beer belly and a scarf wrapped around his cheery face, and his unshaven companion with very short, scruffy white hair poking out from under a baseball cap. They quickly dismissed them and went on with their chatter.

A young waiter approached. He wore tight black jeans over his skinny legs and his hair was half shaved and half in a ponytail. 'Good morning, gentlemen. Can I take your order?'

Richard kept his head down and looked at the front page of the *Daily Mail*. Kevin ordered two lattes with extra shots.

The waiter wrote the order down. 'Anything to eat? Toasted teacake?'

'No, thank you,' said Kevin.

The waiter peered over Richard's shoulder and read the headline. 'I wonder what's happened to him. He came down here once. I never saw him but my mum did.'

'What was he like?' asked Richard in his English accent.

'She said he looked old but still nice.' The boy pushed his notebook into the front pocket of his low-slung apron. 'Two coffees coming up.'

When the waiter had left them, Richard asked, 'How bad are the other papers?'

'Pretty bad. Front page of all the tabloids, the *Telegraph* and the *Guardian*.'

'What's the mood?'

Kevin opened the *Mirror* and scanned the story inside.

'They're saying your disappearance is the biggest mystery since Agatha Christie ran off. They're concerned about you. They think you might have had a breakdown, or run off with a lover, or gone stark staring mad.' He put the paper down and picked up another. 'The *Sun* has a reward for information leading to your discovery.'

Richard perked up. 'Really? How much?'

'Two tickets to your new film and dinner at Gordon Ramsay's place with the *Sun*'s film critic.'

The waiter arrived with their coffees. As Richard stirred his, Kevin asked, 'Look, mate, if you want to go back, just say the word. But for what it's worth, I think you need this time just to get real again. I'll stay with you as long as you need me and do whatever you want.'

Richard looked up from his coffee. 'Really?'

'Yeah. I like a little adventure in my life. Something to tell the grandchildren. And anyway, you can't go anywhere until your hair has grown back again.'

Richard was grateful for the friendship of this kind and honest man and began to relax again. So far no one had noticed him, so maybe he could just disappear for a little while longer. 'I owe you, Kevin,' he said.

'You sure bloody do. Fish and chips, clothes shop and this coffee.'

Kevin reached over and swatted Richard with the rolled-up *Mirror*. 'I'm joking, you silly sod. What are friends for?'

Richard smiled. 'You've saved my sanity.'

'Oh, don't go bleeding soft on me. There are mackerel to catch and pints to be drunk, and they aren't going to do it by themselves.'

Kevin left some money on the table with a hefty tip to avoid any chat with the waiter and got Richard outside.

'Have you ever had a pasty?' he asked.

'My friends Penny and Simon tried to feed me one once, but I managed to dodge it.'

'You don't know what you've missed.'

They walked down the narrow cobbled street that led to the harbour, following the smell of onions, warm pastry and butter as they got closer to the Trevay Pasty Shop.

The front window was piled high with pasties of every size and flavour. Vegetarian, curry, lamb and mint, cheese and onion. Kevin pulled Richard in.

'Two large traditional steak pasties, please,' he said to the lady behind the counter.

'Anything else, my love?' she asked as she

expertly slipped them into two paper bags and twisted the ends.

'Two takeaway teas, please.'

Richard was staring at the cakes behind the glass counter. 'Can we get two doughnuts as well?'

The woman nodded and slipped those into another bag, while she waited for the teabags to brew in the plastic cups.

'You going fishing?' she asked. 'Only the boat's leaving in a couple of minutes. Wouldn't want you to miss it.'

'We're not booked,' Kevin said. 'But do you think there'd be spaces?'

'Ask the skipper. He's coming for his pasty now.'

Chapter 6

In through the door loomed a tall man with dark curly hair which was slightly greying at the temples. He had a thick gold hoop in one ear and was wearing a large, faded, red fisherman's smock. Behind him trotted a self-important Jack Russell terrier.

He nodded at the two men. 'Mornin'.'

Richard nodded back.

The woman behind the counter wrapped up a pasty and made a coffee without being asked. As she handed it over she said, 'Piran, these two gents might like to fish with you today if you've got a space.'

Piran looked them up and down. 'Got your own rods?'

'Not with us,' said Kevin, picturing them leaning by the back door of the caravan.

'No worries, I can hire you a couple. Bait's extra. We're out for four hours, mind. Good sailors, are you? Only it's a bit lumpy out there today.'

Kevin looked at Richard and Richard said, 'What happens if we get sick?'

'Nothing.' Piran laughed. 'You just puke over the side.'

'Well, what's stopping us?' said Richard with a knowing smile.

Piran ignored him. 'You coming or not?'

Richard and Kevin shrugged. 'Yes.'

'My boat's the one down there on the right-hand side. Can't miss her. *LulaBelle Jack*. Follow the dog.'

He gave a brief order to his little dog who trotted off with Richard and Kevin behind him. He was a good guide and directed the men straight to the boat.

LulaBelle Jack had a red hull with blue edges, and a wheelhouse in the stern. Sitting hunched in the bow were three men, in their thirties. All of them were looking green.

'Good morning,' Richard said in his best English voice as he stepped aboard.

'Morning.' They smiled weakly.

Piran climbed on. 'Morning, lads. I hear you're on a stag do. Is that right?'

'Yes,' they mumbled.

'Thinking better of it now, are you?' asked Piran as he started up the engine.

If they replied, no one heard it over Piran's

laugh. 'You'll be fine. If you need to puke, do it over the side.'

He cast off the ropes and motored the little boat out into the open sea. Trevay soon disappeared behind them.

Piran got out his coffee and pasty, and invited Richard and Kevin to join him in the small wheelhouse and eat their pasties there too.

'So what do I call you two?' he asked.

Kevin thought for a moment, then shouted above the noise of the engine, 'Kev and Dick.'

'Nice to meet you. I'm Piran. The dog is Jack. He's a bugger.'

'I have one called Butler.' Kevin grinned. 'We were going to call him Carpenter because he was always doing little jobs around the house.'

Piran chuckled and took a bite out of his pasty. 'It'll take about forty minutes to get out to the fish. There's a lot out there. A lot of mackerel and whiting, but we might get a pollock or bream.'

He whipped the wheel around as he spoke, cresting a tall wave and sliding down it with a thump. 'Told you it was lumpy.'

A groan came from the front of the boat where all three men were now hanging over the side.

'Don't worry about them. They'll be fine once we get back,' Piran said with a wink.

When he had finished his tea and pasty, Richard found a comfy place between the side of the boat and a lobster pot. He wedged himself in and drank in the fresh air and the freedom. No one would find him out here. He closed his eyes and soon fell asleep.

The roll of the sea and the silence woke him. He looked around and saw a cornflower-blue sky above and Kevin sleeping beside him.

The little boat's engine idled quietly.

Piran had left the wheelhouse and was pulling rods and tackle from under the wooden bench seats.

'Here we go, lads,' he said to the three stags who were also waking up. 'This is what we came for.' He handed rods to the men. They had started to look a bit better, but then looked a bit worse again when they were passed a bucket of fish guts as bait.

'There's a lot of fish waiting for you.' Piran laughed as he walked back towards Richard and Kevin, and got them set up with rods and bait.

Kevin got the first catch. A pollock.

Piran was unimpressed. 'Not big enough,' he said. He unhooked the wriggling fish and tossed it back into the sea. 'You have to give that little tiddler back.'

The stags caught a few mackerel, and cheered themselves with cans of beer pulled from their rucksacks.

'I wouldn't drink on an empty stomach if I was you, boys,' Piran advised. 'Especially when I turn the engine off.'

He went to the wheelhouse and shut down the motor. Instantly the noise of the exhaust spitting seawater and diesel fumes stopped. There was silence.

'That's better,' he said. 'You might find the swell a bit hard to stomach at first, but you'll get used to it.'

The lads at the back tried to stand, but they were looking so green that Piran took pity on them and handed them an apple each. 'Eat one of those. It'll help. And if that doesn't help, over the sides, please, gentlemen. Them's the rules.'

They all had bouts of seasickness, including Richard and Kevin, much to Piran's amusement. Even so, they pulled in a good catch.

'Well done, boys,' said Piran, starting the engine. 'You've done good.'

The journey home was quicker than going

out. The tide was coming in and the waves pushed the little boat home.

As they tied up at the harbour, the winter sun was low and there were dark clouds building on the horizon.

The stag-party boys left the boat gratefully.

'Cheers, mate. Nice one.' They shook hands with Piran and carried their catch proudly up to the harbour wall.

Piran shouted after them, 'The Golden Hind does a decent pint and I recommend the curry.'

The three men laughed and gave Piran the thumbs up, then headed towards the ancient pub.

Richard and Kevin began to say goodbye but Piran stopped them. 'Have a drink with me. I got brandy and lovage and you shall have some with me.' He opened up a large canvas bag and pulled out a flask and three plastic mugs. 'Get this down you. Cheers.'

The men drank, and the warm brandy, sweetened with the lovage, was just what they needed.

'Now then,' said Piran, settling himself on the skipper's seat. 'What you doing here, Richard Gere?'

Chapter 7

Several thoughts flashed though Richard's head. Should he deny it? Should he come clean? Should he make a run for it? He looked at a startled Kevin for help.

Piran spoke first. 'No point denying it. I knew it was you the minute I saw you in the pasty shop.' He held his hand out to shake Richard's. 'Piran Ambrose. My girlfriend is best mates with your friend Penny Leighton. The vicar's wife.'

Richard dropped his English accent. 'You're *the* Piran? My God, I've heard so much about you from Penny. What's your wife's name again?'

'Helen, and we ain't married.'

Richard continued. 'Helen, yes. She's adorable. I tried to phone Penny this morning, but then we saw the papers and it kind of took my mind into another place.'

Kevin was worried. 'If you're thinking of telling anyone that Richard is here, you'd better think again.'

Piran smiled his pirate's smile. 'Or what?'

Kevin looked Piran squarely in the eyes and said darkly, 'I know people.'

Piran almost laughed. 'Are you threatening me? Because you have nothing to worry about. I'm all for telling the world to piss off.'

Kevin relaxed his shoulders and looked between Richard and Piran. 'Well, that's all right then.'

'Good.' Piran slapped his hands on his thighs and pushed himself out of his seat. 'How about you two boys help me put the boat to bed and then we go and have a pint? I think a planning meeting is needed.'

The afternoon was cooling rapidly now and the clouds were growing thicker on the horizon. Piran studied them. 'High winds and rain coming in tonight.'

Richard was impressed. 'A fisherman's instinct?'

'You could say that,' said Piran. 'Or you could say I listen to the radio.'

The three men left the boat and walked towards the harbour car park. Kevin hoped they'd be going into the cheerfully lit warmth of the Golden Hind, but Piran walked past it. 'I'll not take you in there. Reporters have been buying locals drinks to get them to talk. We'll go to my house.'

Piran led the way out of Trevay in his battered old red Toyota truck with Kevin and Richard following. After a few miles of ever-narrowing lanes, Piran swung his truck down a track with a dead-end sign on the corner.

He parked on a verge of muddy grass beside a gate and a path leading to a small cottage. He got out as Kevin parked behind him.

Jack jumped down from the truck and went off to sniff out a perfect spot in the hedge in which to cock his leg.

Entering the dark cottage, Piran turned on a couple of lamps to reveal a living room that clearly belonged to a man.

'Come in. No need to take your shoes off.'

Two cats stretched themselves out on the sofa where they had been napping. Yawning, they jumped down and curled around the visitors' legs. 'The tabby is Sprat, and the black-and-white one is Bosun,' said Piran, bending to stroke them. 'Hello, lads. You been good boys? Hungry, I expect?'

Jack shot through the front door and scattered the cats before licking at Piran's hands, wagging his tail in a frenzy.

'OK, boy,' Piran said. 'Dinner coming right

up.' He waved at the sofa. 'Take a seat while I feed the lads, and then I'll get you a pint each.'

From the comfort of the sofa, Richard and Kevin looked at their surroundings. The slate floor was covered mostly with a threadbare Persian rug, but where it wasn't, there was a mass of muddy paw prints. The droopy ceiling was low beamed, and grey with years of log smoke from the open fire.

'You boys know how to light a fire?' Piran called from the kitchen.

'Sure,' replied Richard.

'You'll find all you need in the box by the logs,' Piran called back.

Richard took off his coat and baseball cap, and arranged newspaper and kindling. He found the matches and before long a satisfying blaze was growing.

'Put the television on if you want,' Piran called again. Kevin found the remote and pointed it at the screen. The television was balanced on top of an old lobster pot. Jack's basket and a pile of old newspapers were on the floor. By the front door was a range of outdoor boots, and a shoe box with fishing tackle spilling from it. Kevin sighed with pleasure. What he wouldn't give to live in a place like this.

'Do you want anything to eat?' asked Piran, bringing in six bottles of beer. 'I've got eggs and bacon. It's a long time since we had those pasties.'

Richard, still kneeling by the fire, stood up. 'As long as you let me cook it. Do you have any pasta?'

'Not unless Helen has bought some,' said Piran, settling himself in a big leather armchair.

'I was thinking I could do a carbonara?' said Richard.

'Go and have a look. Help yourself to anything you can find.'

'Will Helen be joining us?' Richard asked.

Piran chuckled. 'We don't live together. She'd drive me mad. Always tidying up. We are happy because she has her house and I have mine. She's round Penny's tonight. The pair of them are worried about you. It's all they can talk about. And here you are, cooking me pasta.'

'I ought to tell them I'm safe,' Richard said.

Piran took a swig of beer. 'You get our tea on and we'll talk about it after. Can't think straight on an empty stomach.'

Richard enjoyed cooking, and to do so in Piran's ancient, but fairly clean, kitchen was fun. Opening the cupboards, he found fishing reels next to sauce bottles. There was a car battery in the larder, and a freshly shot, unplucked pigeon on the draining board.

He opened the fridge. Three bottles of beer, milk, a slightly mouldy lump of Cheddar, six eggs and a packet of bacon.

Under the sink he found the bag of pasta.

As he cooked, he made friends with the cats and Jack, who hovered around him waiting for crumbs of cheese.

Finally, the pasta was ready and he laid the wobbly kitchen table with plates and cutlery and called to the room next door. 'Dinner is served.'

The carbonara was praised, and the last three bottles of beer from the fridge were drunk as the conversation veered from football, to fishing to Brexit and Trump.

Finally, they had to talk about Richard's situation.

Piran began. 'Right. What's the plan?'

Richard groaned. 'The plan was just to get the hell out of that god-awful film and find some peace and quiet. I needed – need – a break, but I had no idea it would turn into such a big deal.'

Piran's phone rang. He excused himself and picked it up. 'Hello?' he barked.

It was Helen, his girlfriend. 'Hey, how are you?'

Piran raised his eyebrows at Kevin and Richard and mouthed her name to them. 'I'm fine. Where are you?'

'At home. I've just come back from Penny and Simon's. There are a couple of reporters still camped outside the vicarage. It's horrible. They've been there all day, knocking on the door and peering through the windows. I had to sneak in and out through the back door and across the churchyard.'

'So there's no news on Richard then?' asked Piran, winking at Richard and Kevin.

'No, nothing. But suppose he tries to get down here and see Penny? Or me? Or Dorrie?

Piran put the phone on speaker to let Kevin and Richard hear. The three of them were feeling very guilty. Richard for starting all this worry. Kevin for his part in the pretence, and Piran because he didn't like to lie to Helen.

'Helen, listen to me,' he said gruffly, 'I want you to come over to my house, it's important that I show you in person.'

'Darling, I'm much too tired for all that to-night.'

Richard and Kevin stifled smiles.

'Not that,' said Piran uncomfortably. 'I've got something here you'd want to see.'

'Can't it wait until tomorrow?'

'Well yes, but I think you'd really like to see it tonight.'

'Piran, I'm tired. I'm getting ready for bed.'

'Just bloody come, woman.' He hung up.

Chapter 8

Helen was not the kind of woman you could order around. She had been, when she'd been married to Gray. But after almost twenty-five years, two children and endless lies about his affairs, she'd divorced him and become her own woman.

She looked at her phone. How dare he hang up? If he thought she would run round to him like a good little girlfriend, he had another think coming. She couldn't imagine what must be so important that she had to drop everything right now. It was dark out and the wind was picking up. She was ready to get into bed and watch an episode of a drama she'd been following. And anyway, she had enough to do with trying to calm Penny over Richard's disappearance.

Penny had always been a drama queen. That was probably why she was so good at her job. Her television production company, Penny Leighton Productions, was doing well, partly thanks to Richard working with her a few years ago on *Hats Off, Trevay*.

Helen smiled at the memory. Who would have thought that Hollywood superstar Richard Gere would have heard about the local fund-raising to save the run-down Pavilions theatre in Trevay? But he had, and he'd helped to turn the whole story into a successful film.

And poor Queenie. Almost ninety and the queen of the Pendruggan village store. She had been running the box office for the theatre when Richard Gere had come in and asked for a ticket. She'd turned him away because that night it had been sold out. Later, when she'd found out who she'd turned away, she'd been so embarrassed. When she did at last meet Richard, he had been lovely to her and spoiled her with his charm.

When Helen had bumped into her earlier, she had been shocked at how concerned Queenie was. 'I feel it, in my water, that he's close to us,' she had said, in between coughs and lighting another cigarette. 'He's here in Cornwall, I just know it. Why doesn't the poor boy give us a ring? He's not in any trouble, and if he is I'll help him out of it.'

Helen had done her best to soothe her, but even Helen's nerves were on edge with the press hanging around the village.

She'd phoned Piran for a bit of moral support,

but typically he'd wanted her to do something for him.

Well, she wasn't going to. She was off to bed. Turning the downstairs lights out, she walked up the stairs of Gull's Cry Cottage and climbed into her large bed to watch her television programme.

Across the village green in the vicarage, Penny was making herself a hot water bottle. What a day! If it felt this bad to her, how must Richard be feeling? It was awful to think of her friend in trouble. She looked out into the back garden and could see Simon, her husband, checking around with his torch. She waited for him to come in, so that they could lock the back door together.

'Any reporters or photographers still there?' she asked him.

'They're not there now, and I don't think they'll be back tomorrow,' he said, sliding the top and bottom bolts into place.

Penny wrapped her arms around herself and gave a little shiver. 'What makes you think that?'

Simon took her hand and spoke quietly, 'Because they know I'm not going to be stupid enough to talk to them again. I've said all I'm going to say.' He switched the kitchen light out and led Penny up the stairs. 'Things will be better tomorrow. I promise.'

Over at the Dolphin pub, Dorrie and Don were busy. The pub was packed. As well as the usual locals, there were reporters who were easy to spot. The men were braggers and the women were wheedlers. But they were all looking for gossip. Pathetic! Dorrie had taken pleasure in turning down the bundles of twenty-pound notes they'd promised her if only she would give them a story. The positive side was that they did drink a good bit and, being hungry, ordered plenty of food. The takings were looking good. As the saying goes: Every cloud has a silver lining.

Chapter 9

Back at Piran's, the boys were enjoying themselves. A good fire was burning in the old fireplace, and the cats and Jack the dog were lounging on the rug, soaking up the heat.

Piran was talking fishing, and his two guests were listening hard.

'Take us out tomorrow,' said Richard. 'I want to catch a conger eel.'

Piran shook his head. 'We got to go at night to get a conger.'

'OK, we'll go tomorrow night.' Richard drank the last of his beer.

'I'll tell you who's a great conger man,' said Piran. 'Don at the Dolphin.'

Richard rubbed his chin. 'I know Don. Penny and Helen introduced us when we were filming. Remind me what his wife's called?'

'Dorrie.'

'How is she?'

'Just the same.' Piran smiled. 'She were a cracker when she was younger.' He looked at his empty bottle of beer. 'I don't know about you boys, but I could do with another one of these. Only we don't have any left.' Piran looked at his watch.

'Let's go to the pub for another drink, I'll drive,' said Kevin. 'I've only had one.'

'What about Helen? Won't she be cross to come over here and find us gone?' asked Richard. 'Give her a call and tell her to meet us in the bar.'

Piran grunted. 'She's bloody not coming now. Awkward woman, she is. Well, she don't know what she's missing, does she?'

The three men stood up and found their coats, patting various pockets for wallets and keys. As Piran slammed the front door, only Jack bothered to cock an ear before settling back down to a warm sleep.

Chapter 10

They had a fun night at the pub, and it was drizzling as they dropped Piran off at his cottage. The wind whipped his dark curls as he walked up his front path.

'Good night,' he shouted, his words blown like scraps so that Richard and Kevin hardly heard them.

For the first mile or two, the road to the Rocky Cliffs Holiday Park was sheltered by high Cornish hedges. But, as it climbed towards the sea, it became more exposed. The rain started to rattle on the windscreen in gusts. The wipers coped at first, but soon began battling to keep the screen clear. As the road reached the top of the cliffs, a gust of high wind side-swiped the heavy car and almost pulled the steering wheel from Kevin's hands.

'Whoa,' he said under his breath. He looked over at his passenger. Richard was asleep.

Kevin drove slowly and quietly through the gates of the sleeping holiday park, with only his side lights on so as not to wake anyone. He could just make out the ribbon of wet tarmac as it headed through the rows of dark caravans. The dry-stone walls around each pitch gave some shelter from a sea breeze on a summer's day, but not from the roaring wind that was coming in tonight.

Cornish palm trees, planted along the way, were bending, their leaves flying at right angles to the grass.

Finally, he pulled up outside his own caravan. The buffeting wind was making it rock. He heard the creak and yaw of the axles. He wasn't too worried. A static caravan was a heavy piece of kit.

Richard woke, blinking beside him. 'Are we home?'

A fresh torrent of rain battered the car's roof.

'We'd better make a dash for it,' said Kevin. 'One, two, three . . . Go.'

The caravan door was almost ripped from Kevin's hand as he opened it, but he hung on and got them both inside. He flicked a switch and light flooded the compact space.

Once inside, he turned on the small radiators and checked that the bedroom was set up for Richard.

'Here's your room. I'll be next door.'

'Home sweet home,' said Richard, yawning.

'What a day.' He gave Kevin a hug. 'Thank you for everything.'

'I'm enjoying it.' Kevin smiled. 'See you in the morning.'

Kevin couldn't sleep, and it wasn't just because of the narrow twin bed he was lying on. The wind was picking up, he was sure of it. The whining, then howling, then screeching as it chased itself over the ocean and around the Rocky Cliffs was worrying him. He could hear the sea, the waves thumping onto the shore, and their vibrations rippling through the thin walls of his mobile home.

He got out of bed and crept into the lounge. Peering through the curtains, he saw broken branches and leaves flipping and rolling in front of him, scudding up the path from the beach.

He looked to his left and saw the roof of the caravan next to him pulling and rattling against the gale.

He'd never seen it like this before.

He found June's radio by her armchair. It was tuned to BBC Radio Cornwall, as usual. He sat down, turning the volume down so as not to wake Richard, and held the speaker to his ear.

'. . . many power cuts over the county as the high winds pull down electricity lines. A spokesman for the energy company says that many more homes are likely to be affected. And we have just heard that the Trevay lifeboat has launched after a fishing vessel sent out a Mayday call at around 2.30 a.m. The details are as yet unknown. Meanwhile, the Met Office gale warning remains in place, but they say the storm is due to blow itself out by mid-morning tomorrow . . .'

Outside, a terrible roar of metal grating against metal had Kevin leaping to his feet.

Richard appeared beside him. 'What the hell's going on?'

A ripping, wrenching, sickening roar and the sound of breaking glass answered them.

'I think the roof next door has blown off.' Kevin was searching for a jacket. 'Stay here.'

Chapter 11

Outside, the horizontal rain stung the bare skin of Kevin's throat and ears. He hunched his shoulders against it and screwed up his eyes. He saw a scene of havoc. The wind had torn two roof panels from the older caravan next door. They were cart-wheeling up the slope beyond him. He watched as they snagged on a clump of palm trees, then flew up and over a hedge to continue their journey of destruction.

He prayed that no one was in their path.

Another, more powerful gust buffeted against him and almost knocked him off his feet. He heard the sound of more grating metal.

He watched, dumbstruck, as a third piece of roof was ripped off and hurled at the large window of a caravan no more than twenty metres from him. He shut his eyes and waited for the crash of glass smashing.

He opened his eyes and saw the piece of roof embedded in the window. Shattered glass shimmered like frost all around.

A pair of rose chintz curtains were now swaying in the empty frame and, above the howl of the storm, he thought he heard a voice.

He ran towards the caravan and shouted, 'Hello? Is there anybody in there?' Reaching the front door, he tried the handle. Locked.

He listened again.

Richard arrived, dripping wet and breathing hard.

'Shh,' Kevin said. 'I think someone is in there.'

Both men listened, hardly breathing.

'There,' said Kevin. 'Hear it?'

'I'm not sure,' said Richard.

Kevin ducked his head as another squall of rain hit them full on. 'We'll try the back door.'

The wind was coming from behind them now and knocked Richard forward to his knees, and he slid on the wet ground. He winced with pain, then got to his feet. 'Shit,' he said, feeling the sting of gravel on the palms of his hands.

Kevin turned round. 'You OK?'

'Sure.'

Kevin reached the back door and tried the handle. It was unlocked.

The savage wind immediately whipped the handle from his grip and pinned the door to the outside wall of the van, narrowly missing Richard's fingers.

Kevin was already inside the caravan. It felt like a mad fairground ride. The floor was rocking under his feet and the wind was running from the smashed window to the open back door.

'Hello?' he called. He fished in his jacket pocket, hoping his phone was in it. It was. He turned the torch on.

'Bloody hell,' he said.

The narrow corridor to the back bedroom was blocked by a piece of roof that had caved in. The night sky was swirling above him.

'Help me with this!' he shouted to Richard.

It wasn't heavy, but it was awkward and sharp on their cold hands. And it refused to move. Richard pointed to the ceiling. 'Look!' One corner was still bolted to the roof. 'We'll have to try and bend it out of the way.'

Using brute force against it, they finally began to make the metal give way. After what felt like for ever, it folded back enough for Richard to reach the bedroom door. Kevin held the weight of the twisted roof against him. 'I'll hold this. It wants to spring back. You go and get them out. But be quick. It's heavy.'

Richard gave him the thumbs up above

another howl of wind, and pushed open the door.

Inside the small bedroom he found a young couple, in their night clothes, huddled on the bed. Their state of distress – and now relief – was clear.

'Come on!' shouted Richard. 'Let's get you out.'

The young man pushed his wife towards Richard, who helped her out into the corridor and past a sweating Kevin.

Richard turned, expecting to find the young man behind him, but there was no sign of him. He looked at Kevin, who was straining under the weight of the metal. 'You OK for another minute?' Richard asked. Kevin nodded.

Richard hurried back and found the man. 'Come on. You've got to get out of here. Now.'

He saw the young man bundling blankets together. 'Leave that. Come on!' he shouted again.

'It's the baby,' the man shouted, handing the bundle to Richard. 'Take her out.'

A blast of wind hit the caravan, pulling at the remaining panels of the roof.

Richard took the baby and the man's arm. They went out into the corridor, past Kevin, and outside to where the young woman stood drenched and shaking in the storm.

Richard handed the baby over, then ran back to Kevin. He grabbed Kevin's arm and pulled him outside, to safety. The straining metal snapped back sharply as soon as Kevin's weight was lifted.

The caravan was now creaking and rocking violently.

'Run!' shouted Richard.

They ran, turning only when they saw the final bits of roof and all the walls blown off and away into the darkness.

Chapter 12

The rescuers and rescued ran against the wind and down to the safety of Kevin's caravan. It was still standing.

Kevin opened the door and helped them in. 'I'll put the fire on. Richard, put the kettle on, and you two,' he nodded towards the young couple, 'get out of those clothes and have a hot shower. I'll get towels.'

'I was scared,' said the young mum, still clinging to the bundle of baby. 'I thought we were all going to blow off the cliff.'

'It's all right now.' Her husband hugged her to him. He turned to Kevin and Richard. 'Thank you.'

Richard poured hot water into four coffee cups. 'Get this down you.' He passed them round. 'I'm Richard.'

'I'm Paul and this is Katie.'

Richard peeked into the baby's bundle of blankets. 'And who's this?'

'Rebecca,' said Katie. 'She's only six weeks old.'

Richard smiled. 'Well, she seems to have slept through the whole drama.'

Kevin came back with a pile of towels and some clothes he thought might be unisex. 'Probably too big for you, but trackie bottoms and hoodies OK?'

'We are very grateful,' said Paul.

'Shower's running. Who's hopping in first?'

Outside the storm was beginning to subside.

Richard insisted that the little family had his double bed. 'Kevin has twin beds in his room. I'll bunk in there,' he said. 'You don't mind, do you, Kev?'

Outwardly, Kevin didn't seem worried. 'No problem.' He grinned.

Inwardly he was panicking. June was always moaning about his snoring. And now, here he was, bunking up with a Hollywood actor. Who'd believe it?

'You go on ahead. I'll just clear up here.'

He spent as long as he could washing up the coffee mugs and folding wet clothes, but eventually he had to go to bed. He hoped Richard would be asleep. He wasn't. He was propped against his pillow, his chest bare, cleaning his glasses.

'What a night,' Richard said, running his hands through his stubbly hair. 'Life with you is never dull, Kevin.'

'Hah. No.' Kevin's brain was whirling. How

many clothes should he take off before getting into his tiny bed? The space between the two of them was about half a metre. He'd have to reverse into the bed, so as to avoid sticking his backside into Richard's face. He shimmied out of his jumper and T-shirt, then quickly dropped his jeans, thanking June for packing some decent pants. He went in from the bottom of the bed, head first, under the duvet.

He popped out at the top end, pretending this was perfectly normal.

Richard was looking at him and raised his eyebrows. 'You've still got your socks on.'

'Umm . . .' Kevin was rescued by the sound of knocking on the door. He got up, wrapping the duvet around him.

It was Paul, wanting to say thank you again and let them know the shower was free.

Richard appeared at the doorway in a hastily pulled-on jumper and shorts. 'Is everything OK?'

Kevin explained and Richard clapped Paul on the back, telling the young man not to worry.

Paul looked at Richard more closely. 'You look awfully familiar.'

Kevin looked from one to the other nervously.

'Really? I must have one of those faces,' Richard said, shrugging.

Paul looked at him and shook his head. 'Must be all this stuff about what's-his-name, that actor. That's not you, is it?'

Richard held his hands up. 'Nope. Not me.'

Paul smiled and opened the door to go back to his wife and baby. 'Just as long as you know how grateful we are.'

'We do. Good night.'

''Night.'

Kevin closed the door behind him.

'I thought the game was up then,' he said.

Richard laughed softly. 'Come on. I'm an actor. We've got to get some sleep if we're to be any help tomorrow. June told me you snore.'

Chapter 13

Morning broke as if nothing had happened. The sky was blue and clear. The sea shone like a mill pond, and the breeze was as gentle as the beating of the wings of an early butterfly.

Richard woke to the hungry cries of baby Rebecca coming through the paper-thin walls.

He looked over at Kevin's bald head shining on the pillow. If he'd snored at all last night, it hadn't disturbed Richard.

Richard stretched his arms over his head and yawned and thought about the day ahead.

No schedule.

No lines to learn.

No emails.

Bliss.

He was looking forward to putting in some physical effort and helping to tidy up the holiday park. But first, he needed a pee.

He rolled out of his tiny bed and stood up.

His knee hurt. Looking down he saw the graze and large bruise from when he'd fallen in the wind last night. He tested his weight on it again and limped to the loo. Washing his face and hands, he saw the blood on the heels of his palms where he'd tried to save himself from falling. They stung as he soaped the grit out.

He looked into the steamed-up mirror and inspected his unshaven face. 'Danny Zuko's grandfather,' he said solemnly, remembering his role in *Grease*.

He wrapped a towel around his waist and went to the kitchen.

Katie and the baby were sitting at the table – Katie with a cup of tea to her lips, Rebecca with a breast to hers.

'Oh, pardon me,' said Richard, embarrassed. 'Would you rather I . . .' He pointed back to the bedrooms.

'I don't mind, if you don't.' Katie adjusted a muslin cloth to give Rebecca privacy.

He began to make a pot of tea. 'Did you sleep OK?'

Katie nodded, then winced as Rebecca wriggled and started to grizzle. 'She don't latch on too well,' she explained.

'Oh. Aha,' said Richard, not looking. 'Shall I take a tea in to Paul?'

'Wake the lazy bugger up,' said Katie.

Carrying two mugs, Richard woke Kevin first.

'What's the time?' asked Kevin groggily.

'About nine, I think.'

Kevin pulled himself up the bed and ran a hand over his stubbled chin. 'What time did we get to bed?'

'About three?'

Kevin muttered a curse and took the tea.

'This is for Paul,' said Richard, looking at the tea in his other hand. 'Katie is up and feeding the baby.'

Kevin didn't bother to answer. He swigged his tea and kept his eyes tight shut.

In the room next door, Paul was asleep, his mouth open with a thin string of drool joining him to the pillow.

'Paul,' Richard whispered. 'Tea here. By your side. OK?'

Nothing.

Richard hovered in case there was a response. Still nothing. Only steady breathing. 'OK. Well, you sleep, and I'll see you later,' Richard said, backing out of the snug room.

In the living area, Katie was pacing up and down with Rebecca, who was chewing her fists and bleating.

'Is she still hungry?' said Richard, collecting his mug of tea.

'It's always like this. I can't give her what she needs,' Katie said.

'Yes, you can.' Richard hesitated.

Katie started to pace again. 'I tried. With the midwife and the health visitor. I'm going to start bottle-feeding soon.'

'Do you want to bottle-feed?'

'Not really, but I can't let her go hungry.'

'You just need a little time.'

'I've done six weeks.'

'That's nothing. You just need to sleep. You must be exhausted. Here, I'll watch her while you get some rest.' Richard cradled Rebecca in his arms and she was immediately soothed, her little face looking up at him adoringly.

When Katie woke up from her nap, Richard had put the kettle on.

'Cup of tea?'

As the kettle boiled, Paul came in, and Katie told him how Richard had helped her and Rebecca.

Richard carried the tea over.

'Cheers, mate,' said Paul, 'and thank you for, you know, helping my missus.'

'Don't mention it. Want a cookie?' Richard went to a cupboard and pulled out a packet of biscuits.

Katie laughed. 'Them's not cookies. That's a biscuit.'

Chapter 14

The caravan park was a mess. Kevin was standing on his steps gazing at the wreckage.

The park owner had been up all night, and was now driving a man from his insurance company around in a golf cart to inspect the damage. The young couple had got an early start and had headed home already.

Richard came outside and stood next to Kevin. 'Morning.'

'Morning.'

'I hope the owner of the park is well insured,' said Richard.

'Why?' Kevin gave him a mocking look. 'You going to rescue this place too?'

Richard raised his eyebrows and said in Texan drawl, 'Honey! You think I'm made of money?' He tilted his face to the thin warmth of the sun. 'Come on, then. You and I are going to help clear up this park.'

At the ornate iron gates to the park, cars and volunteers were gathered.

The owner of the park was welcoming each group and quietly giving instructions.

Richard saw Don and Piran standing by Piran's truck. He and Kevin walked towards them. 'Hi,' he said. 'What a night.'

'We got no power in Pendruggan,' said Don. 'One of those big trees up the lane to Trevay fell on the line.'

'Is Dorrie OK?' asked Kevin.

'Yeah. She's fine.' Don shoved his hands in his pockets. 'She's going to open up the pub anyway. She says you two are to come back for lunch if you want it. Only sandwiches, mind.'

The owner of the park approached them. 'Can you lot sort out the damaged caravans? Make the glass safe and collect any roof metal?'

'Sure,' said Piran. 'We can chuck it in the back of my truck. Where do you want us to dump it?'

'A couple of skips will be here soon.' The owner smiled at the men and then he looked at Richard. 'Good of you to help.'

Richard tugged his baseball cap a little lower over his eyes. 'Happy to help.'

Piran distracted him. 'Right, let's get the job done.'

As Piran, Don, Richard and Kevin got into

the truck, a Volvo estate swept through the gates and blocked them in.

Piran swore. 'It's the vicar. Keep your head down, Richard.'

Simon leapt out waving at Piran. He came towards the truck and stuck his head through the open driver's window. 'Community spirit. Isn't it wonderful?' He greeted Don sitting in the passenger seat then turned his gaze to the back seat.

Richard stared back at him.

Simon took a sharp breath. 'Oh, my Good Lord.'

'Ssh,' said Piran. 'Don't say a word.'

Simon stood up and looked around, as if to check that no one was listening, then bent through the window again and whispered, 'Penny and Helen will be here in a minute. They're bringing Queenie with some pasties for the helpers. They're bound to see you, and you know they won't be able to hide their surprise. And with all these people here, they'll accidentally give Richard away.'

Just then, Helen's smart little Mini appeared through the gates. It headed for Simon's Volvo.

'Move your car,' hissed Piran, turning his truck's ignition key.

Simon jumped in front of the Mini as it pulled

alongside. 'Sorry, Helen, you're going to have to reverse back. I need to move the Volvo. Piran needs to get the truck down to the worst of the damage.'

The four men worked hard over the next two hours, bantering all the while.

Piran made six journeys to the skips and each time managed to avoid the women.

On the seventh he was stopped by Helen. She planted herself firmly in front of him. 'Are you ignoring me? Is it because I didn't come over last night?'

He kissed her cheek and tried a jolly smile. 'Hello, my bird. Not at all. I was glad you didn't in that storm. Let me get this done and then I'll see you at home later.' He tried to get past her but she walked with him.

'Wasn't it awful? My windows were rattling and the garden's a mess. Perhaps you could help me clear it up at the weekend?'

Penny waved to them both from the door of the camp-site shop. 'We've set up a canteen. Tea, coffee, Queenie's pasties. Dorrie's coming later with sandwiches,' she shouted.

Piran groaned, then quickly smiled again. 'That's lovely. But I need to get this job done, then I have to go directly home.'

'Well, pop in on your way home,' Penny called to him. 'I'm assuming you have no power, no electric?'

'No. Maybe. I've got stuff to . . . er . . . check on,' he said.

Penny waved again and went back to her work.

Helen pulled a face of concern. 'Is the cottage damaged? You said you were going to fix those roof tiles weeks ago.'

'Yeah, yeah. I'm a fool.' He was humouring her now. He put his arm around her shoulder and turned her back to where she'd come from. 'You've got to keep feeding the troops. I'll drop in for a cuppa later, or I'll see you back at yours.'

Don, Richard and Kevin were sweeping the last traces of damage away as Piran returned. 'Right, lads,' he said. 'Get in the truck and keep your heads down. The whole bloody gang of women are up there dishing out tea and sympathy. We've got to get by without them stopping us. They will notice who you are and the secret will be revealed to everybody.

'I could do with a cuppa,' said Kevin.

'Or a coffee maybe?' said Richard.

Don turned to look at them on the back seat. 'I'd kill for a bloody pasty.'

Piran rammed the truck into reverse and started a three-point turn. 'We are not stopping up there. They'll be on Richard like a pack of dogs.'

He turned the wheel. 'Right. Let's get out of here.' He put his foot to the floor and headed up the hill, leaving the sea behind them.

'What the bloody 'ell?' Piran hit the brakes.

A very old lady in a sagging fur coat, woolly hat and thick glasses was standing a few yards up the road, flagging them down. She was carrying a bulging Tesco 'Bag for Life'. 'Keep down, Richard, or we'll never get away.'

Piran unwound the window and said rather more cheerily than he felt, 'All right, Queenie?'

''Ello, me duck. Saved you some of me home-made pasties. Good job I've got me gas cooker. Mind you, it's terrible cold at my place. All the electrics have gone off. Last night I slept in me coat.' She stroked the ratted fur. 'Lucky I had it. Church jumble sale, twenty year ago. Fifteen pounds, but you can't put a price on quality.'

Queenie handed the bag through the window. 'One for you and one for Don. Here, Don, your Dorrie has just arrived with some lovely sandwiches.' She had almost her entire upper body in the window now. 'You two have done a lovely job, ain't you? I said to Helen and Penny, them boys will be wanting one of my pasties.' Her eyes shifted to the back seat. Under the brim of his hat Richard could see the smears of grease on the lenses of her huge glasses.

'Who you got in the back there? Introduce us, then.'

Piran dropped his head onto his chest and sighed. 'A bit of a surprise. When I tell you, you must promise not to scream or attract attention. Understand?'

She stuck out her whiskery chin. 'No names, no pack drill. That's me motto. From the war.'

Piran nodded and took a deep breath. 'It's Richard and his friend Kevin.'

'Richard who?'

Piran coughed and waited until a small group of volunteers had gone past. 'Richard, Richard.'

Queenie's face was blank. Then the meaning of Piran's words began to sink in. She stuck her head even further into the car and craned her neck to see into the back seat.

Richard took his cap off. 'Hi, Queenie. Long time no see.'

Chapter 15

Queenie's wide eyes narrowed. She coughed her wheezy cough, then smiled. 'Well then, I'd better get another couple of me pasties.' She opened the back door of the truck. 'Squeeze up.'

Richard and Kevin squeezed up.

She nodded at Kevin. 'How do.'

'Hi.'

'All right, Richard?' she asked.

'All the better for seeing you.' He smiled.

She put her mottled hand into Richard's and gripped it. 'You'll be all right now, son.'

Piran drove to the entrance of the holiday park and stopped just before the gates. Queenie let go of Richard and slowly unfolded herself from the truck. 'I'll just tell the girls we need two more pasties,' she said. 'Stay where you are.'

In the shop, there was a small queue waiting for teas and coffees and filling paper plates with Dorrie's sandwiches.

Queenie bustled in. 'Excuse me, ladies and

gents.' The people stopped and listened. 'I shall have to ask you to leave. We need to close for a short while. Open again in fifteen minutes.'

Penny was puzzled. 'We don't need to close, Queenie.'

'Oh yes we do,' said Queenie firmly, giving them an urgent look. 'You need a break. The law says so. You've been on your feet for hours.' She rested her hands across the front of her fur coat and, with raised eyebrows and a strong stare, she willed them to obey her.

Helen got the message. 'Yes, we could do with a short break. Thank you, Queenie.'

The group of volunteers didn't complain. They gathered their snacks and went outside. Queenie shut the door behind them and turned the 'open' sign to 'closed'.

'What's this about?' asked Helen.

'Listen up.' Queenie was feeling like a general addressing his troops. 'What I'm going to tell you now is top secret.'

Penny, Helen and Dorrie looked at each other and then back to Queenie. 'OK,' said Helen slowly. 'What is it?'

Queenie winked. 'Richard is in Piran's truck.'

Helen and Penny were dumbstruck.

'Where?' Dorrie managed to say.

'Outside. In Piran's truck. Have a look if you

don't believe me. But try to look calm, for gawd's sake.'

Penny, Helen and Dorrie went to the glass door and looked out.

Piran and Don waved from the front seat and, in the depths of the back seat, they could just make out the handsome, smiling face of their old friend.

Penny sighed with relief. 'He's safe.'

Helen was thinking back to the night before. 'That's why Piran wanted me to go over last night.'

The four women looked again towards the truck outside, then spun around as they heard the back door of the stock room creak open. 'Hellloooo?' called Simon's voice. 'Penny?' He appeared through the door of the stock room. He stopped and looked at the four expectant women. The deep freeze clicked and began humming.

'Oh. Hi. Everything all right?'

'Do you know who's in Piran's truck?' asked Penny.

Simon wasn't sure how to answer this. He did know, but perhaps he should pretend he didn't? He decided that truth was the only way.

'Yes.'

Penny tightened her lips. 'Who?'

Simon felt that he may have fallen for a trick. He shuffled his feet and leant one hand on the humming freezer. 'Erm . . . Do you know?'

'Answer the bloody question,' Penny snapped. 'Do you bloody well know who is in Piran's bloody truck?'

'Yes. It's Richard.'

Penny banged her fists on her thighs. 'So everybody knew but me? Why did nobody tell me?'

'Or me,' said Helen crossly.

'Or her,' shouted Penny.

'Well, I haven't seen you since I found out,' said Simon. 'I was coming now to tell you, but you all seem to know, so . . . no harm done.'

Penny made a growly sound in the back of her throat and turned to look out of the window again.

The freezer stopped humming.

'Well,' said Queenie. 'I've only come to get a couple of pasties.'

She went to the thermal glass box that was keeping them warm. She found two plain paper bags and, rattling them open, popped a pasty in each. 'Right you are.' She went to the door and turned the 'closed' sign back to 'open'. 'Now we all know, what are we going to do about it?'

Penny set her chin and said quickly, 'We have two spare rooms at the vicarage. Richard and his friend can stay with us. Simon, go outside and tell Piran to drive straight there. They can follow you down and you can let them in.' She glanced around at the others. 'Dorrie, I want you and Don there. The staff can run the pub.'

Dorrie nodded. 'I'll let them know.'

'Helen, you and Piran could pick up a take-away curry. Richard likes chicken tikka, as I remember. Is that OK with you, Queenie?'

'I'll have a poppadum but nothing too hot,' said Queenie.

'Right,' said Penny. She was enjoying being in charge. 'The vicarage in two hours. Then we'll decide what to do.'

Chapter 16

The power had come back on in Pendruggan by the time Richard was smuggled into the vicarage. He was wearing Simon's clerical cloak and a panama straw hat.

They needn't have bothered. All the journalists had vanished. The new big story was the storm damage across the whole of southern Britain.

Kevin and Don returned to the caravan to collect the luggage.

Simon showed Richard up to the best spare room. 'The en suite is in here. I think you could do with a bath.'

Richard smiled his slow smile.

'Not that I think you need to.' Simon was flustered. 'I'll get you some towels.'

'It's very kind of you and Penny. I am so happy to be here again. Three days ago, all I wanted was to be here, and now I am.' Richard stretched his arms wide and fell backwards onto the bed. 'Jeez, this bed is comfortable.'

'Shall I get you a coffee? Tea? Glass of wine?'

'I think I'll get in the tub and then take a nap. We had a long night last night.'

'Yes, yes. Terrible. Shall I close the curtains for you?' Simon moved to the window but Richard stopped him.

'Simon. I'm fine. I'm really happy.'

'Yes. Good. It's just that . . .' Richard smiled, pulling his lips down instead of up. 'I'm trying to make sure that everything is done as Penny would do . . . before she comes home.'

'Don't worry. I'll tell her you were the perfect host.'

'Right. OK.' Simon went to the door then turned. 'Shall I wake you, in time for supper? In case you fall asleep?'

'Simon, get out!'

'Yes, yes. Of course. Sorry.' Simon went out and closed the door behind him.

Richard stayed on the bed and stretched. Within moments he was sleeping.

'But, how long has he been asleep?' asked Penny, wiping the breakfast crumbs from the sink. 'The takeaway will be here any minute.'

Simon was laying the big kitchen table with cutlery and glasses. 'I don't know.'

'You must know.' She reached for the roll of kitchen towel to use as napkins. 'What did he say?'

'That he was going to have a bath and a nap.'

'And I have done those things and I feel terrific.' Richard was lounging against the kitchen door jamb, looking freshly bathed and smelling divine. Penny reached for him and hugged him as tightly as she could. 'God, it's so good to see you. I've been worried sick.'

Simon was ripping the paper towel into sheets and tucking them into the wine glasses. 'We've all been worried.'

The back door opened. Don and Kevin came in carrying a couple of bags and a yellow ruck-sack. 'Here we are,' said Don. 'Where shall I put these?'

'Pop them in the hall, darling,' said Penny. 'And you must be Kevin?' She kissed his cool cheek.

'That's me. Minder to the runaway stars.'

Simon offered wine or beer, while his guests milled about finding the right chair to sit on.

'I want to hear exactly what happened and what you've been up to, Richard,' said Penny, making sure she sat closest to him.

She was interrupted by the back door opening again and letting in the cool air. 'Hello, hello,' said Helen. She was carrying a large box of hot tinfoil boxes. Piran came behind her with a crate of Skinner's beer and plonked it on the side.

Helen made a beeline for Richard and hugged his head to her bosom. 'God, we were so worried about you.'

'I've told him that,' sniffed Penny.

'You smell so good too,' said Helen, inhaling Richard's cologne and ignoring Penny.

Piran got between the two women and handed Richard an opened bottle of beer. 'Cheers,' he said.

'Cheers,' said Richard, clinking Piran's bottle.

'Penny,' Simon called from the other side of the table, 'give me a hand with the food, would you? I don't know what's what.'

Penny tutted. 'For goodness' sake, Simon. It's not rocket science.'

'I know, but you recognise what's what. I'll get it wrong.'

Penny got up and beckoned Helen. 'Will you help me?'

'I'm talking with Richard.'

'Well, so was I.'

The back door opened again, and Dorrie and Queenie came in. 'There he is,' cackled Queenie. She was still wearing her fur coat. 'Saved a seat for me, did you?' Queenie could move like lightning when she wanted to. She was in Penny's seat almost before Penny had left it.

'Up you get, woman,' Piran growled to Helen. 'Richard and I have things to talk about.'

Over supper Richard managed to get his story out with Kevin's help and many interruptions.

Penny and Helen, who had both been pushed to the far end of the table, listened eagerly.

'So what happens next?' Simon asked, handing Richard another bottle of beer.

'I would like to stay a little while.' Richard looked at his friends' faces. 'I like it here and want to spend time with you. Until you get bored with me, or I'm found.'

'We'd love you to stay,' said Simon. 'Wouldn't we?'

Everyone nodded in agreement.

'But you can't stay locked up in the house all day,' said Penny. 'You need things to do.'

'There's a chimney come down in the village,' said Don, chewing at the remains of his naan bread. 'The scaffold's gone up this afternoon. I'm working on it tomorrow. How are you up ladders?'

'Pretty good,' said Richard. 'I'll help.'

Don swallowed his naan down with a swig of beer. 'If I thought that was true, I'd be happy to have you.'

'It is true,' said Richard. 'I did a lot of labouring to pay my way through college.'

'And how long ago was that?' Don asked.

Richard gave a wry nod. 'Before the War of Independence.' Everyone laughed. 'Seriously. I like construction. I built a barn once.'

Don looked at Richard, wondering. 'Are you having me on?'

'No, sir.'

'You good up ladders?'

'Sure.'

'What you doing tomorrow?'

'Fixing a chimney.'

Chapter 17

The next morning, Pendruggan woke to clear blue skies and the warmth of the morning sun.

Richard drew the curtains in his bedroom at the vicarage and watched the jackdaws as they jostled for position on the church roof, their waxy feathers gleaming in the sun.

He leant on the windowsill and switched his gaze to the garden below. Crystal drops of dew hung on the silver threads of cobwebs stretched across the old yew hedge.

A robin hopped on the battered bird table looking for breakfast crumbs that had not yet arrived.

He smiled and treated himself to a deeply satisfying stretch. He took his time, pulling every sinew in his neck, shoulders and hips. It was the perfect day for climbing roofs and fixing chimneys.

In the kitchen, he found Simon and Penny in deep discussion.

'If only Audrey would let the Young Farmers

get on with it instead of all this arguing.' Simon was fretfully polishing his glasses. 'I'm a clergyman but I accept that Valentine's Day has nothing to do with the modern Christian church these days.' He placed his cleaned glasses on his nose and took Penny's hand. 'Am I wrong?'

'Absolutely not. Audrey Tipton is *the* first-class witch of this parish. She is intent on spoiling anybody and everybody's fun. You must stand up to her.'

Simon smiled weakly. 'She's terrifying.'

'Remember David and Goliath,' said Penny, patting his hand.

'Hey,' said Richard, 'anything I can do?'

'Morning,' said Penny. 'Would you like a coffee?'

'I'll fix it.' Richard went to the kettle.

'No, you won't,' Penny insisted. 'Simon, make Richard a coffee. A proper one. And I'll have one too.'

'So what's going on?' Richard asked, sitting himself opposite Penny.

'The Valentine's fundraiser for the Holy Trinity youth club. Audrey Tipton has been running it for years, but this year the Young Farmers, all of whom were once members of the youth club, want to make it more exciting.

Apparently, the usual raffle and fish-and-chip dinner is no longer to the taste of the Pendruggan youth. Not to mention dancing to the Geoffrey Tipton Toe Tappers.' She sighed. 'Who can blame them? Geoffrey Tipton – Audrey's husband – and his portable organ with drum and bass are no substitute for Ed Sheeran.'

'They have raised a lot of money over the years,' said Simon, spooning fresh coffee into the percolator.

'Oh yes,' snorted Penny. 'Last year just about covered the cost of the hall hire.' Simon handed her a coffee. 'Thank you, darling.' She took a sip and said with some malice, 'Geoffrey's portable organ needs the chop.'

Richard was thinking. 'Ed's a sweet guy.'

Penny widened her eyes. 'You know Ed Sheeran?'

Richard nodded. 'Sure, I know of him. I have his music on my phone.'

Penny clutched her chest theatrically. 'For a moment there . . .'

There was a tap on the back door. 'Come in,' called Simon.

'Morning.' It was Don. 'Is my labourer ready?'

Richard drained his coffee and got to his feet. 'Yes, sir.'

* * *

The air was cool and dry as they crossed the village green towards a cottage covered in bottle-green ivy, and scaffolding.

Richard followed Don round the back and saw the damage for himself. The chimney had lost several bricks from the top and was tilting towards a small conservatory below. Several slates were missing from the roof, exposing the timber rafters.

'Can you mix mortar?' Don asked, tipping his head towards Richard.

'Show me exactly how you want it and I'll do it,' Richard replied, smiling.

It was fun. Richard enjoyed the fresh air and the purpose the simple work gave him.

As the church clock struck one o'clock the last chimney brick was tapped into place. The conservatory below was safe again.

'How about a pint at the Dolphin?' said Richard. 'On me?'

'We've still got those slates to fix,' Don replied, 'but we can do them after some lunch.'

'So is that a yes?' asked Richard.

'Aye.' Don slung his padded tartan jacket over his narrow shoulders and walked towards his Rascal van. 'Hop in.'

* * *

After lunch and a pint at the Dolphin, Richard and Don returned to their work for the rest of the afternoon. Their only interruption was the arrival of Kevin in his Jaguar, with Penny and Helen as passengers.

'Just taking these two ladies into Truro for the afternoon,' he explained. 'We'll be doing a bit of shopping, and I'm cooking tea tonight. See you later.'

Richard smiled as they drove away. Another wave of calm swept over him. A wave of belonging to this friendly, funny community. He knew it couldn't last, but while it did he was grateful.

Kevin lifted his grocery bags onto the table and began to unpack them with Penny's help. A couple of bottles of wine, a six-pack of beer, a whole chicken, an assortment of vegetables and a newspaper. 'I checked the papers,' Kevin said to Richard. 'Nothing. Nothing on the news neither.'

'I think you've managed to disappear very successfully.' Penny held up a bottle of beer. 'Fancy one of these to celebrate?'

'Yes, please.'

Penny opened the bottle and passed it to him. Richard stood up. 'I'd like to make a toast to good friends and kindness.'

Penny filled her wine glass. 'It's our pleasure. We'd like you to stay for ever.'

'Buddha teaches us that nothing is for ever,' said Richard.

'Well, thank goodness for that,' said Kevin. 'Now, how do you fancy roast chicken and all the trimmings for your tea?'

'Well, that was an excellent dinner,' said Simon, leaning back in his kitchen chair. 'Where did you learn to cook like that?'

'The army,' said Kevin. 'Seven years, and it's true, soldiers do march on their stomachs.'

'Where did you serve?' asked Penny.

'Iraq. Afghanistan.' Kevin shrugged.

'You are a quiet one.' Penny smiled. 'Brave too.'

'We had our moments.'

'Thank you,' said Simon. 'For telling us and for cooking for us.'

Kevin smiled and stood up. 'Anyone for apple crumble and custard?'

The phone rang.

Sighing, Simon went to answer it. 'Hello, Pendruggan vicarage.'

A woman's voice boomed down the line. 'Simon? It's Audrey Tipton. I need to speak to you about the youth club fundraiser.'

'It's quite late,' Simon suggested, looking at his watch.

'Yes. I shall be with you in ten minutes.'

'Well it's not very con—' Simon began, but Audrey had already hung up. He went back into the kitchen. 'Audrey is coming over.'

Penny was eating her apple crumble. She swallowed quickly. 'Now?'

'I'm afraid so.'

Penny scowled and shook her head.

The doorbell rang.

Chapter 18

Simon went to the front door wiping apple crumble from his lips with a sheet of kitchen towel.

Audrey Tipton pushed herself through the door. Her husband, Geoffrey, followed.

'I thought we'd pop round before we have our dinner,' she bellowed. 'Geoffrey has made one of his fish pies. It's in the oven, so while it's heating we can get some things straight about the youth club fundraiser.'

She bustled down the hall to the kitchen, Simon and Geoffrey following behind.

'Audrey!' said Penny over-brightly as she tried to clear the table.

'Mrs Canter.' Audrey had never approved of the vicar's choice of bride. Her beady eyes surveyed the dirty dishes on the table. 'You eat early? How rustic.' She stared at the other people in the room – two men she didn't recognise. She took in their workmen's clothes and uncombed hair.

Kevin and Richard smiled warily at her.

She ignored them and sat down. 'Let me get straight to the point,' she barked. 'I am not prepared to waste my valuable time on a Valentine's shindig. Its Christian associations are long gone and now it's just disgraceful. It could lead to all sorts of sinful activity. Nicotine, alcohol, heavy petting . . .'

Penny stifled a laugh. Audrey glared at her. 'You think it's funny, Mrs Canter?

'Not at all.' Penny coughed. 'But neither do I believe a Valentine's party will stunt anyone's spiritual growth. We need to admit to the dark side in order to recognise the light side. Don't we?'

Mrs Tipton's eyes widened then narrowed to burning slits. The broken veins on her cheeks began to throb.

Richard – feeling it wasn't his place to witness this local dispute – scraped his chair back and stood up. 'If you'll excuse me, I'm going to take a shower.' He put his hand on Kevin's shoulder. 'Come on, Kev, let's leave these good people to sort out their differences.' Kevin couldn't get to his feet fast enough.

Once the two men had left the room Audrey inhaled deeply, expanding her vast bosom.

Penny wondered if flames were about to be breathed on her.

She was almost right.

'The dark and the light?' Audrey smirked. 'Good and Evil? Ying and Yang? Is that what you are referring to?'

'Yes,' said Penny firmly.

'Ha,' Audrey snorted. 'That's exactly the sort of thing I would expect from a loony lefty Londoner.'

Simon, who had been leaning on the kitchen cupboards, stepped forward. 'Now, Audrey, there's no need for that. This is not about politics. It's about fun.'

Geoffrey chipped in from the safety of the kitchen door. 'Audrey believes in tradition. And there's nothing wrong with that.'

Penny banged her hand on the kitchen table, making Simon jump. 'Valentine's *is* a tradition.'

Audrey stood up and bent over Penny. 'No, it is not. Tradition is Geoffrey playing toe-tapping tunes on his portable organ.' As her voice rose so did her hand, pointing her finger towards her husband. 'Geoffrey's organ has entertained thousands over the years and he's not going to stop now.'

Penny stood too and pushed her face closer to Audrey's. 'I beg to differ. I have been in this parish for more than six years and I have never once been entertained by Geoffrey's organ. It has become a joke. It may have struck the right note in 1972, but not any more.'

Audrey gasped like a mackerel on a hook. 'Geoffrey!' she shrieked. 'Say something!'

Geoffrey was white and looked close to tears. 'Don't speak to my wife like that,' he managed.

Simon, ever the peace-maker, put his palms up in surrender. 'It's late and I'm sure that things will look different in the morning, and we can come to some kind of agreement.'

'Why not do it now?' Richard strolled in, freshly showered and smelling divine. Audrey gaped at him.

'I know you.'

'How do you do,' he said, offering her his hand. 'Richard Gere.'

Audrey fell back into her chair.

'Oh my,' she said, flustered and blushing. 'I loved you in *Pretty Woman*.'

'Thank you,' said Richard, sitting down next to her. 'Simon and Penny are under a lot of strain. You may have read that I have vanished?'

Audrey gulped. 'Yes.'

'Well, I came here. To see old friends. I needed to ground myself with real people for a while.'

'Yes, yes. I quite understand.'

'And now I have involved you and your charming husband in my pretence.' He looked at Geoffrey. 'Mr Tipton, can I rely on you and your wife not to tell anyone where I am? I feel I can trust you both.'

Audrey gazed at him with doe eyes. 'Of course you can, can't he, Geoffrey?'

Geoffrey puffed himself up. 'Naturally. Mum's the word.'

Richard smiled. 'I am hugely grateful. And because of that I would like to offer my services to the fundraiser.'

Penny and Simon sat down too. 'How?' asked Simon.

'Geoffrey?' Richard looked at him. 'Do you know the score to *Grease*? And if not, how fast could you learn it?'

'Well, I am pretty good at sight-reading.'

'What is *Grease*?' asked Audrey.

'Oh, it's a very famous musical that was turned into a film with John Travolta and Olivia Newton-John.'

'I've always liked her,' breathed Geoffrey.

'Shut up,' ordered Audrey. She said softly to Richard, 'Why are you telling us this, Mr Gere?'

'Please call me Richard.' Richard touched Audrey's hand. 'I can teach you the dances, and then you can teach the kids on the night? Maybe a little *Rocky Horror Show* too? I'll bet you do a fine "Time Warp"?' He looked deeply into Audrey's piggy eyes. 'Or I can teach you?'

'Teach me,' she said huskily.

Still locked onto Audrey's eyes, Richard said, 'Penny, can you find the soundtrack to both pictures?'

'Certainly.' Penny was loving his work. 'I'll get my laptop.'

In the vicarage sitting room, Penny hurriedly pushed the chairs and sofa aside to create a makeshift dance floor. She logged on to the laptop and downloaded both *Grease* and *The Rocky Horror Show*.

Simon came in. 'My God, Richard is hypnotising her,' he whispered.

'I know. Great, isn't it? Open the lid of the baby grand and get them in here.'

Richard was holding Audrey's hand when they walked in. Geoffrey, rather put out, was sulking.

'Geoffrey,' said Richard, 'perhaps you could play along on the grand piano? Can you play by ear?'

'I have perfect pitch,' he blustered.

'Well, that's great.' Taking Audrey's other arm,

Richard said over his shoulder, 'Penny, play "Greased Lightning" for us.'

Penny found the track and pressed play.

It was late by the time Geoffrey managed to drag Audrey away. He had bleated for the last hour and a half – 'My fish pie will be ruined!' – while Audrey had ignored him. Fuelled by a hefty gin and tonic – 'Just a small one, please' – she had lifted her tweed skirt and danced in her stockinged feet. Richard was the perfect partner. He held her just close enough and helped her hips to move in ways Geoffrey had never seen, or experienced.

'Oh, my dear,' she had gasped, dizzily, 'I had no idea of the creative nature of pop music. I am a very creative person. Sensitive to the arts.'

Richard caught her around her waist and pulled her to him. 'And such innocent fun.' He grinned.

The music stopped and Richard released her. He bowed and kissed her hand. 'You are a great dancer.'

'Well,' said Audrey, almost fluttering her sparse eyelashes, 'one is only as good as one's partner.'

Geoffrey was tapping his watch. 'My fish pie?'

Penny struck while the mood was still hot. 'So, what about the Valentine's party?'

Geoffrey was collecting up Audrey's jacket and hat. 'We'll think about it,' he said.

'I've thought about it, and yes, the youth club may have a Valentine's party.' Audrey paused, making certain she had her audience at her will. 'But, there shall be no unsuitable costumes. By that I mean no spare flesh on show.'

'Totally understood,' said Simon, beaming.

Geoffrey was now forcing Audrey's unwilling arms into her jacket. 'My old organ may not be much, but I'll do my best learning those tunes,' he said.

Richard leapt forward to help. 'Geoffrey, I think you and your organ deserve a night off this year. Why not let the youngsters DJ a bit of their own stuff? Hm?'

'Quite so,' said Audrey. 'I'm not sure you'll play the way the music is supposed to be played.'

If Audrey had struck Geoffrey across the face, he could not have looked more wounded. 'But . . .' He looked to the others in appeal, but no eye met his. He looked at his shoes and swallowed. Penny thought he was on the brink of tears. 'Very well,' he managed. 'Come along, Audrey. I'm afraid the fish pie is ruined. It's cheese on toast for us.'

* * *

Penny, Simon, Richard and Kevin stood at the front door and waved the Tiptons off. 'She's pissed,' said Penny under her breath. 'How much did you give her, Simon?'

Simon shrugged one shoulder and tapped his nose.

'And you a vicar.' Penny kissed him lightly. 'Another small miracle.'

Simon looked at Richard. 'It was all your doing. Thank you.'

'My pleasure, but could you please shut the door? I need to sit down and have a drink. She has heavy feet.'

Chapter 19

The following morning, Simon walked up to the village stores. Queenie, ancient postmistress, shopkeeper and first-class gossip, was the best person to tell the good news to.

'Morning, Queenie.'

'Morning, vicar.' Queenie was behind the counter sitting on an armchair of unknown age with a two-bar electric heater at her feet. She was doing a crossword by the light of an old table lamp which always sat on the counter. 'Practise magical tricks. Something O something something U something E.' Her whiskered lips moved over the top of her biro like an old horse eating a Polo mint. 'Any ideas?'

Simon enjoyed a crossword, but his real errand needed attending to first. 'Let me think.' He furrowed his brow. 'Oh by the way, I'll bring the tickets over in a day or two for the youth club fundraiser.'

Queenie took the biro from her mouth and replaced it with one of her roll-ups. 'I won't sell many. Them bloody Tiptons ruin it for the young 'uns.'

'Ah, well, I have news.' Simon quickly explained.

'Oh, my good Gawd.' Queenie gave one of her crackly laughs. 'That Richard could charm a bloody worm from a tree, couldn't he?' She laughed again. 'Old Tawdry Audrey Tipton fell for his game good and proper, didn't she? Silly old bat.' Her cigarette was hanging in the right-hand corner of her lips, defying gravity. She took a long suck on it, and squinted her eyes to avoid the smoke pluming from her nostrils. 'Bring as many tickets as you can. We'll raise a lot this year.'

'Excellent.' Simon turned to go but at the door he turned. 'Conjure,' he said.

'Eh?'

'Practise magical tricks?'

'Oh, let me see.' She studied her crossword through her spectacles. 'So it is. Cheers, vicar.'

'Cheers, Queenie. Spread the word about the Valentine's disco, won't you?'

Simon left the shop whistling. The blue skies of yesterday were now obscured by cloud and a chill wind was blowing, but he decided to take a walk around the village green before returning to the vicarage. It was a peaceful scene. The cottages grouped around the large oval green, a tractor bumping over the cattle grid heading for the top field, a lone cat sitting on the bench by the phone box washing itself. Simon sent a prayer of thanks for the many blessings he had been given.

As he reached the far end of the green, Simon heard angry voices. He stopped to see who it was. Coming towards him down the lane from the Dolphin pub was Don, marching angrily away from Dorrie, who was almost running to catch him up.

'Don't you walk away!' she was shouting. 'Just typical of you. You can't take criticism, can you?'

Don stopped in his tracks and turned to face her. She stopped running and stood still.

'I don't know what's wrong with you, woman!' he shouted back. 'Nag, nag, nag, that's all you do. You're turning into a right misery and I don't want to be around you right now.'

Dorrie promptly burst into tears and ran back towards the pub.

Don shook his head and ran his fingers through his hair as if to tear it out.

'Can I help?' Simon asked, walking nearer. 'I

couldn't help overhearing.' He could see that Don was fuming.

'Bloody woman.' Don kicked a piece of turf at the side of the lane.

'Ah. Marriage is not easy all the time.'

Don was clenching and unclenching his fists. 'I can't take all this anger in her. I'm told I'm lazy. That I don't care about her. That I'm useless around the house. Nothing pleases the woman.'

'Mmm.' Simon nodded, thinking of Penny.

'Bloody mood swings. It's her age. Time of life. I keep telling her to go to the doctor but she won't listen.'

'Ah,' Simon understood.

'I'm going for a walk. Clear my head,' Don huffed.

'Care for company?'

'Yeah, all right.'

'I just need to drop in at the vicarage to get my coat.'

In the vicarage, Penny was on the phone in her office while Richard and Kevin were lying on the sofa watching *Homes Under the Hammer*. Simon popped his head round the door.

'Just going for a walk with Don.'

'Where to?' asked Kevin, not looking away from the reveal shot, which showed that a once-derelict cottage had become a glamorous family home.

'Um, the beach, I think,' said Simon.

Richard looked up. 'I'd like to see the beach.'

Before Simon could stop him, Richard had turned the television off and was dragging Kevin off the sofa. 'Walk will do us good.'

Simon went outside and saw Don picking at a scab on his finger. 'Do you mind if Richard and Kevin join us?' he asked, worrying that Don would mind.

Don looked up. 'Might take my mind off that woman I'm married to.'

'Oh yes?' asked Richard as he and Kevin came out of the house. 'What's going on?'

The four men walked down the lane to Shellsand Bay and talked as they went.

'Why do they get so damn stroppy?' asked Don. 'One minute they're the girl of your dreams, next they're man-haters.'

'Not man-haters,' said Richard. 'They're just sensitive to things.'

'Like what?'

'They like to feel appreciated. To be considered. How often do you thank Dorrie for the clean pants that are always in your drawer?' Richard asked.

'Of course I appreciate her. She knows it.'

'But do you tell her?'

'She don't need telling.'

Kevin had been listening carefully, and now he butted in. 'Me and June had a bad time about five years ago. She'd never minded me working all the hours in the day, but suddenly she got all difficult about it. I couldn't do anything right.'

Simon nodded. 'I do feel that, some days when I get home, I find I have failed an exam I didn't know I was taking.'

They came to the end of the lane and walked out onto the wide sand of the beach. The tide was coming in. The onshore breeze blew the spray into their faces, forcing them to sink their necks even further into their coats.

Richard picked up a stone and sent it skimming. 'All women need is a kind word. A cup of tea. A question about their day.'

'Really?' asked Don. He looked doubtful.

'Really. Possibly the offer of a foot rub too.'

'Oh yes,' Simon piped up, 'I've found that that really does work. On Penny, anyway.'

'And,' continued Richard, 'if that doesn't work, ask them how they feel about their lives.'

Don shook his head. 'I'm not a bloody counsellor, I'm her bloody husband.' He picked up a stone and lobbed it into the waves.

Richard patted him on the back. 'I'm just saying. Try it. You might be surprised.'

Don picked up another stone and weighed it in his hand, thinking, before chucking it into the ocean. 'I dunno.'

'How about we come to the pub for a pint tonight, to give you moral support?' Kevin suggested. He liked the idea of a night out.

'If you like,' Don said glumly.

Penny opened the front door to Simon, Richard and Kevin before Simon had his keys out. 'Come in quickly,' she said, looking flustered. 'There's a strange car to the right-hand side of the green. Don't look.' She dragged Simon back from the hall window. 'Green Toyota. Two men. They arrived after you left. They drove by the house a couple of times, and they've been sat over there ever since. I've got a funny feeling about them.'

Kevin nudged Simon and said under his breath, 'Press, do you think?'

They watched as Richard took his coat off. 'I could do with a coffee,' he said. 'Penny, can I get you one?' He winked at his friends and took

Penny by the hand. 'Come and sit down. How's your day been?'

Later that day, when Penny was taking the bins out, she glanced across the common to see if the green Toyota was still there. It wasn't. She put her fears out of her mind.

Chapter 20

The usual locals were at the bar in the Dolphin. Piran was at the centre of a group at one end, and the young farmers were at the other, celebrating their Valentine's victory.

'The drinks are on me,' said Richard, striding to the bar while the others found a table by the log fire.

Dorrie was serving but he caught her eye. 'Won't be a minute, Rich,' she said.

While she served her customer, Richard looked around. Richly polished tables and chairs were grouped around, each one lit by a tea light in a jam jar. The bar itself was a beautiful piece of shiny old oak, pockmarked with history and holding an enormous brass bowl with gaudy dahlias spilling from it. The old flagged floor was covered in an assortment of worn and faded rugs. Every now and again, the kitchen door flapped open and shut as a young waitress carried through bowls of steaming mussels or steak and chips.

Dorrie came to him. 'What can I get you?'

'Kev and I will have a pint of Skinner's and . . . Do you know what Simon likes? I forgot to ask.'

Dorrie smiled. 'Yeah, I'll bring 'em all over to you.'

Richard handed over some money. 'Is Don about?'

Dorrie raised her eyes to the ceiling. 'He's in the kitchen. We had a bit of an up-and-downer today. He's trying to be nice.'

Richard raised his eyebrows, pulling down the corners of his mouth at the same time. 'Is it working?'

'A bit.'

'Good.'

At the table the men were talking about surfing. 'I haven't been out since last summer.' Simon patted his taut stomach, 'I need to.'

Piran ambled over and pulled up a chair. 'The vicar is being modest. He could have been a pro if God hadn't needed him here. Ain't that right, vicar?'

Simon polished his glasses, a sure sign he was embarrassed. 'You are very kind.'

Dorrie arrived with Don and a trayful of drinks. 'Here you are, boys.'

'Let me help you with that,' said Don, taking the tray from Dorrie.

'I can manage.'

'I know you can but I'd like to help. You've had a long day.'

Dorrie looked at Don suspiciously, and then at Richard. 'See what I mean?' She put the last of the glasses on the table, then turned back to Don, her hands on her hips. 'Why are you trying to get round me? What have you been up to?'

'Just my way of saying sorry for this morning,' said Don innocently.

'Oh. Well.' Dorrie was puzzled, but gave him the benefit of the doubt. 'Apology accepted.' She pecked him on the cheek and smiled. 'See you later then.'

The men watched as Dorrie, slender and dressed in denim, returned to the punters at the bar.

Don lifted his beer to Richard. 'Cheers, mate. I think it's working.'

Walking back to the vicarage, Richard felt his phone vibrate in his pocket. He'd check it when he got back home. It was too dark to read in the lane, and anyway his reading glasses were by his bed.

Kevin and Simon were walking ahead chatting amiably.

As they came to the village green, Richard

heard a car behind him. He called to the men ahead of him, 'Car coming.'

The car almost coasted past them. Richard saw two figures in the front. It was a green Toyota. Simon and Kevin continued, too busy talking to notice it. Richard watched it slow and come to a stop about fifty yards from the vicarage. The engine died and its lights went out.

Chapter 21

Back in the vicarage, Richard made an excuse to go upstairs. He fumbled for his specs and opened up his phone. A text from his agent, Janie.

You OK? Thought I'd better tell you. They've found you. I'm sending a car to get you out of there tomorrow – 10.00 a.m. Afternoon flight booked. See you tomorrow night in LA. Janie.

PS. I'm sorry.

There was a knock on his door. He quickly closed his phone. 'Come in.'

'Hope I'm not disturbing?' It was Simon.

'Not at all.' Richard smiled wearily.

Simon sat on a small chair, his elbows on his knees. 'How are you?'

Richard's shoulders slumped. 'You a mind reader?'

'I saw the green Toyota.'

'Ah.'

'Penny is worried.'

'Look, you and Pen have been so generous to me. This has been the best time I can remember for a long time. But it has to end. I'm going tomorrow.'

'Tomorrow?' Simon said sadly. 'We'll miss you.'

Richard dropped his head. 'Me too.'

'Do you want to talk to me about what's troubling you?'

In the kitchen Simon poured them both a glass of whisky, before leading Richard to his study and shutting the door. 'Penny is in bed. We won't disturb her in here.'

They took an armchair each.

'Where would you like to begin?' asked Simon gently.

Richard opened up in a way he hadn't been able to for a long, long time. Simon listened carefully and asked the odd question. As the hours slipped by, Simon offered advice and suggestions, but most of all understanding and friendship.

Richard looked back on that night as a turning point in his life. Trevay really was a special place and it proved that good friends, good food and a Cornish getaway were all you needed to see your life in a different way.

*　*　*

Penny pestered Simon for days afterwards to find out what they had talked about, but Simon always replied, 'It is my duty to keep any confidential conversation, confidential.' Eventually Penny gave up.

All she knew was that, when she came down for breakfast the next day, Richard's bags were in the hall.

In the kitchen, Richard was boiling the kettle and humming quietly.

He looked quite different from the scruffy bearded man he'd become over the last few days. He'd shaved, he was wearing a smart shirt with a jumper tied around his shoulders and his trousers looked brand new. She went to him and hugged him. He smelt so clean and fresh. She buried her nose into his shoulder, breathing in his seductive cologne.

'Hey,' he said, holding her. 'What's this about?'

'What's going on? You're not leaving, are you?'

He pulled a smile of regret.

'Oh, God. You are leaving, aren't you?'

'It's time. All things must come to an end.'

'Bloody Buddha again?' Penny said.

'Yeah. Bloody Buddha again.' The kettle boiled and he kissed the top of her head before letting her go. 'Cuppa?'

'Have you got time?' she asked.

'The car will be here in a few minutes,' he told her.

'Is Kevin taking you back?'

'No. My office has organised everything,' Richard said. 'If I don't get out now, your life will be turned upside down by all the press attention. Again.'

The back door opened and Kevin and Simon came in, bringing the smell of fresh Cornish air with them.

'All clear, boss,' said Kevin.

'Great,' said Richard.

'What do you mean?' asked Penny.

Simon went to her and held her hand. 'PC Oaten is outside. He's moved the green Toyota on and his pal is stopping all unknown cars from coming through the village until Richard is safely on his way to London.'

Penny sat down heavily. 'This is crazy.'

There was a bang on the door.

'That's me,' said Richard, walking to the hall.

Penny, Simon and Kevin followed. Kevin picked up the bags. 'Let me get these in the car for you, Rich.'

'Thanks,' said Richard.

On the doorstep PC Oaten stood upright. 'Good morning, vicar. Mr Gere.'

'Morning,' smiled Richard.

Kevin dodged by with the bags as a blacked-out limo reversed onto the drive. The driver got out and helped load Richard's meagre luggage.

'Well. This is it.' Richard tried to sound upbeat. 'See you guys soon, eh?'

He shook Simon's hand before falling into a man hug. 'Thanks for last night.'

Penny looked heartbroken.

'Hey,' said Richard, releasing Simon and holding his arms out to Penny. 'Last hug?'

'Last hug.' Tears were slipping down her cheeks as she held him. 'We'll miss you. Good luck.'

The driver opened the rear door of the limo.

Richard let go of Penny. 'Say goodbye to everyone, won't you? Say I'm sorry I had to go so soon.' He was walking backwards but ever closer to the car.

'Love you guys.'

'Love you,' Penny said, wiping her cheeks.

Richard turned and ducked inside the car.

They couldn't tell if he was waving or not through the black glass, but Penny and Simon waved madly as the car drove out of the drive, around the green and disappeared.

Back inside the house, Kevin, Simon and Penny stood quietly.

Simon reached for his handkerchief and blew his nose. 'A very decent chap.'

Kevin pulled out his phone. 'I'd better call June and tell her I'm on my way home.'

Penny went upstairs.

Richard's room was still and empty. All trace of him gone. Had he even been here?

She pulled the sheets off the bed and threw them in a bundle onto the landing. In the en suite bathroom she picked the damp towels from the towel rail, and then she saw it.

On the glass shelf above the sink.

A bottle of cologne.

His cologne.

Her fingers felt for the glass stopper and pulled it out. She sniffed. It was him.

Yes, he had definitely been here.

When the only place you want to be is home…

THE *SUNDAY TIMES* BESTSELLER

FERN BRITTON

Coming Home

Escape with the new novel from
Fern Britton

22nd February 2017

PROLOGUE

Trevay, 1993

The house was still.

Her heart was hammering – she could hear it in her ears, hear her breath whistle in her nostrils.

She tried to quieten both.

In the dark of her bedroom, she strained her ears to listen for any noise in the house.

The church bell rang the half hour. Half past eleven.

She'd gone up to bed early, her mother asking her if she was feeling all right.

'Yeah. I'm fine.' She'd shrugged off the caring hand her mother had placed in the small of her back.

'If you're sure?' Her mother let her hand rest by her hip. 'Is it your period?'

She had hunched her shoulders and scowled at that. 'I'm just tired.'

'Ella and Henry had a lovely day with you on the beach,'

said her mother, bending her head to look up into her daughter's downcast eyes. 'You're doing so well.'

Sennen shrugged and turned to head for the stairs. Her father came out of the kitchen. 'Those little 'uns of yours asleep, are they?'

'She's tired, Bill,' replied her mother.

'An early night.' Her father smiled. 'Good for you.' She could feel her father's loving gaze on her back, as she ascended the stairs. She wouldn't turn around.

'Goodnight, Sennen,' chirped her mother. 'Sleep tight.'

Her parents had finally gone to bed almost an hour ago and now she picked up the heavy rucksack she'd got for her fifteenth birthday. It had been used once, on a disastrous first weekend of camping for the Duke of Edinburgh Bronze award. Even now the bone-numbing cold of one night in a tent and the penetrating rain of the twenty-mile hike the following day made her stomach clench. Back home she refused to complete any more challenges and dropped out. She used Henry as an excuse. He had just started to walk and her mother expected her to come home from school every weekend and do the things a mother should do for her child. On top of that she was expected to work hard for her exams. Why the hell would she want to learn how to read a map and cook a chicken over a campfire as well?

And then Ella came along.

Sennen had sat in the summer heat of the exam hall, six weeks from her due date, hating the kicks of her unborn child, hating being pitied by her teachers.

She rubbed a hand across her eyes and tightened the straps on the rucksack. What a model daughter she had been. Two babies by a father unknown and now she was leaving. Leaving them, her A levels, her over-indulgent liberal leftie parents who had supported her through it all – and leaving Cornwall.

She hovered on the landing outside Henry and Ella's room. She didn't go in. She knew she would never leave if she saw them, smelt them . . . She kissed her hand and placed it on their nameplates on the door. Downstairs, she tiptoed through the hall. Bertie the cat ran from under the hall table with a mew. She put her hand to her mouth to stop her startled cry then bent down to tickle him. 'Bye, Bert. Have a nice life.'

Slowly she turned the handle of the downstairs loo and edged in carefully, making sure that the rucksack didn't knock over the earthenware plant pot with its flourishing spider plant. Bert came with her and she had to nudge him out with her boot before closing the door behind him. The front door was too noisey to leave by.

The loo window always stuck a little and the trick was to give it a little thump with your palm. She held her breath, listened for any noise from upstairs. Nothing. She wound the small linen hand towel around her fist. It took three good pushes, each stronger than the last before the window swung open, noiselessly.

She threw the rucksack out first and then carefully climbed out after it.

She pushed the window shut and stood in the moonlit, tiled courtyard. In a corner was Henry's little trike and in another, Ella's beach pushchair. She had meant to take both in in case of rain, but had forgotten. She looked up to the night sky. Cloudless. It would be a dry night.

She picked her way over the sandpit, held in a wooden box that her father had made for her when she was little and now given fresh life to with a coat of scarlet paint, and made her way to the gate. The hinge creaked a little, but before it had shut itself she was already gone. Around the corner, down the lane and out to the bus stop by the harbour.

There are lots of ways to keep
up-to-date with all things

Fern Britton

f /officialfernbritton

🐦 @Fern_Britton

www.fern-britton.com

About Quick Reads

Quick Reads are brilliant short new books written by bestselling writers. They are perfect for regular readers wanting a fast and satisfying read, but they are also ideal for adults who are discovering reading for pleasure for the first time.

Since Quick Reads was founded in 2006, over 4.5 million copies of more than a hundred titles have been sold or distributed. Quick Reads are available in paperback, in ebook and from your local library.

To find out more about Quick Reads titles, visit

www.readingagency.org.uk/quickreads

Quick Reads is part of The Reading Agency,
the leading charity inspiring people of all ages and all backgrounds to read for pleasure and empowerment. Working with our partners, our aim is to make reading accessible to everyone.
The Reading Agency is funded by the Arts Council.

www.readingagency.org.uk Tweet us @readingagency

The Reading Agency Ltd • Registered number: 3904882 (England & Wales) Registered charity number: 1085443 (England & Wales) Registered Office: Free Word Centre, 60 Farringdon Road, London, EC1R 3GA The Reading Agency is supported using public funding by Arts Council England.

We would like to thank all our funders and a range of private donors who believe in the value of our work.

LOTTERY FUNDED

THE
READING
AGENCY

Stories about real life

Stories to take you to another time

Stories to make you turn the pages

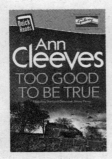

For a complete list of titles visit

www.readingagency.org.uk/quickreads

Available in paperback, ebook and from your local library

has something for everyone

Stories to make you laugh

DEAD MAN Talking
RODDY DOYLE

Two women, one man...
RED FOR REVENGE
Fanny Blake

Looking for Captain Poldark
ROWAN COLEMAN

JOJO MOYES
Paris for ~~Two~~ One

A BABY AT THE BEACH CAFÉ
Lucy Diamond

EDITED BY
VERONICA HENRY
ANNIVERSARY
Ten tempting stories from ten bestselling authors

Stories to make you feel good

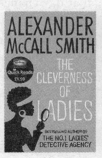

ALEXANDER McCALL SMITH
THE CLEVERNESS OF LADIES
BESTSELLING AUTHOR OF
THE NO.1 LADIES' DETECTIVE AGENCY

Jenny COLGAN
a Very Distant Shore

Stories to take you to another place

Start a new chapter

The Beach Wedding

Dorothy Koomson

Will your past always catch up with you?

Tessa Dannall is excited and happy when her daughter,
Nia, arrives at their family's tropical beach
resort to get married.

Tessa is also trying to forget the last time
she went to a wedding on this beach and how
that day changed her life for ever.

But as the big day draws near, Tessa realises
she must face the deadly ghosts from her past
– or they may ruin her daughter's future.

Start a new chapter

Cut Off

Mark Billingham

It's the moment we all fear: losing our phone,
leaving us cut off from family and friends. But, for Louise,
losing hers in a local café takes her somewhere much darker.
After many hours of panic, Louise is relieved when someone
gets in touch offering to return the phone. From then
on she is impatient to get back to normal life.

But when they meet on the beach, Louise realises
you should be careful what you wish for …

Six Foot Six

Kit De Waal

It's an exciting day for Timothy Flowers. It's the third of November, and it's Friday, and it's his twenty-first birthday. When Timothy walks to his usual street corner to see his favourite special bus, he meets Charlie. Charlie is a builder who is desperate for Timothy's help because Timothy is very tall, six feet six inches. Timothy has never had a job before – or no work that he's kept for more than a day. But when Timothy and Charlie have to collect money from a local thug, things don't exactly go according to plan ...

Over the course of one day,
Timothy's life will change for ever.

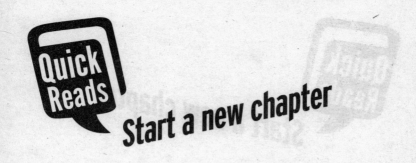

Quick Reads

Start a new chapter

Inspector Chopra and the Million-Dollar Motor Car

Vaseem Khan

A Quick Read from the bestselling author of the
Baby Ganesh Agency series, about an Indian police inspector –
and his baby elephant sidekick.

The Premier No.1 Garage is the place to go in Mumbai
if you want a luxury car. Even Mumbai's biggest gangster shops
there – he's just ordered a classic race car worth millions.

But now the car is gone. Stolen from a locked room,
in the middle of the night.

Who stole it? The mechanic who is addicted to gambling?
The angry ex-worker? The car thief pulling off one last job?

And how on earth did they make it vanish from the locked garage?

Inspector Chopra has just days to find the culprit –
and the missing car – before its gangster owner finds out . . .
and takes violent revenge.

Available in paperback, ebook and from your local library

Quick Reads — *Start a new chapter*

Clean Break

Tammy Cohen

DIVORCE CAN BE DEADLY

Kate wants a clean break from her husband Jack.
They can still be friends. She just doesn't
want to stay married to him.

But Jack doesn't want a friend. He wants a wife.
He wants Kate. And he will do anything to keep her.

Jack remembers his wedding vow:

Till death do us part

He always keeps a promise.

Available in paperback, ebook and from your local library